The Last Book Ever Written
Victor Vale

A novel by

Jonah Kruvant

PANAM BOOKS
Where Words Take Flight

Published by

PanAm Books LLC
P. O. Box 3179
Upper Montclair, NJ 07043
www.panambooks.com

ISBN-13: 978-1-942693-17-8 (print)

ISBN ebook-13: 978-1-942693-18-5 (ebook)

The Last Book Ever Written
Library of Congress Control Number Available

PRINTED IN THE UNITED STATES OF AMERICA

Cover Photo Debra L. Rothenberg
Graphic and Cover Design by Robin McGeever, McB Design

"You can kill a man but not an idea."

Benazir Bhutto

Connie,

Thank you for your support and I hope you enjoy the book!

Acknowledgements

I'd like to thank Peter Golden, Judith Curr, Jason Martin, Hilary Leichter, and Judith Lindbergh for their sound advice; my cover designers, Robin McGeever and Gary Finkler; my photographer, Debra L. Rothenberg; my illustrator, Alison Kruvant; my proofreader, Natalie Maneval; my editing team, Ben Friedman, Matthew Hoch, Dara Kruvant, and Reuben Meltzer; and everyone at PanAm Books, Ingrid Davidsen, Laura Lentin, and especially Roseann Lentin for believing in this book.

I'd also like to thank the following teachers: my eighth grade English teacher, Mr. Ebling, for encouraging me to write; the professors in my MFA program, Darcey Steinke, Susan Kim, and particularly John McManus who is the single greatest influence on this book; and to my mentor, Steven Millhauser, who inspired me to write.

Thank you to my parents and the rest of my family and friends for their love and support. This book is dedicated to my dog, Willy, Uncle Dale, and to my grandmother, the "famous" Naomi Kruvant.

Now forget about me. This story belongs to Victor Vale.

In memory of Sylvester Huppington

Preface

It all starts when we're born. Our mothers take their last pained breaths of labor, our fathers hold us up just long enough to feel proud, and then they do it. They insert the chip into our brains. The computer inside of us. As if we were the automatrons themselves. Until we don't know where the computers begin, and we end. Is it any wonder then, that so many of us are so distant? So … addicted?

Perhaps you've never set foot in the Slums. Perhaps you've only seen them from the skytrain on excursions to the Dancing Towers or The Mountain. Well, I'm a detective. An officer of the law. I go everywhere and see everything. Some things I'm not supposed to see. I've met people I never would have otherwise—beggars, creators … even Lana Lapin. Yes, I even met the President herself.

That's why Sylvester Huppington chose me to write this book. And while it's dedicated to his memory, and inscribed so that future generations will not forget, I wrote it for you. For everyone. For beggars, Upperclassmen, and even members of the Technological Police. Because something has gone terribly wrong in the world. We have to stop it before it's too late.

Part I

The Badge

Chapter One: The Slums

Not long after the Cleansing Act, I was promoted to Detective. I was thirty-four. I had a wife and child to support. A career to pursue. My son wanted things, my wife wanted things; hell, I wanted things. I had worked on the force for thirteen years and it was time I got my detective badge.

That was all I could see back then. I didn't care about creators.

Then I was assigned to the case. But even before I stepped into The Chief's office, events began taking shape that marked both the beginning and the end of a new chapter in my life. It was on my way to the police station, wading through the unbearable stench of the dirty human flesh of the Slums, that I began to question things, what I thought I knew about the world … and about myself.

So this is where I start my story. This is where I begin my book.

That day, for whatever reason, I felt conscious of my surroundings. The beggars were pushing each other out of the way to get under awnings and balconies of restaurants and apartments as it started to rain. The restaurants were filled with shattered glass, moldy kitchens. The strongest beggars lived in cramped apartments with cockroaches and termites. The ones who couldn't find shelter that morning just laid there, shivering from the cold. Some would let raindrops fall from the sky into their open mouths. Two naïve children were chasing each other around bodies and giggling, cleaning dirt out of each other's hair. The bright lights of the skyscrapers, the swiftness of the skytrain, the convenience of the airpath—all a beggar had to do was look up, and he would find himself lost in a fantastical world of dreams.

These beggars would keep their distance from men of the law—they knew that interfering with the police would do them no good. They fed off Upperclassmen who wandered accidentally into their area after a drinking binge or after their cars broke down on the airpath and they had to land in the streets. These beggars, perhaps, were not *always* beggars. They had been street cleaners, maids, waiters. They had jobs before the automatrons were introduced and the National Uprising was squelched. These beggars had a morsel of hope that somehow things could change.

But the beggars who lived deep within the Slums were aggressive and desperate. Some had lived there for generations. They were prone to violence, theft, and seemed nefarious by their very nature. As I came closer to the station, they began watching me with eager eyes. They'd beg for water, food, money, my shoes. The daring ones would call me names. I pretended not to hear them, but I could feel my feet quickening their pace. The beggars seemed not to care about the rain, letting it soak into their clothes as if letting death itself seep into their bones. Their god was food, hunger their religion. One woman, spotting a can of beans, ran from under a balcony to get it, but a half-naked man walking near the can snatched it away from her. She pushed the man to the ground, and the beans scattered everywhere. The woman leapt over the man and started to gather up the beans as people nearby, magnetized by the aroma, crawled toward the beans and gobbled them up from the ground with their mouths like animals.

The most repulsive part of walking through the Slums was not the sights but the smells. A release of the nostrils would let in the stench of feces, decay, and filth, too unbearable to endure for any visitor. But the beggars were used to the smell. This was their life.

I often wondered if people lived this way in other parts of the world. Of course with the restrictions on air flight, I had never been out of The Nation and nor had anyone I knew. I used to think that by joining the force, I'd somehow learn about the outside world. But I never did. For all I knew, we were the only place in existence.

I did hear an occasional police report from other parts of The Nation that no ordinary citizen would ever get a hold of. "Beggar uprising squelched in San Francisco," "Automatron factories built in North Dakota," "Genetically engineered food puts farmers out of work in Nebraska." I was raised in the suburbs with a child's yearning to see the world. But then I grew up. There was no reason to leave The City; all the jobs were here. President Lapin knew that any rebellion of substance would stem from The City. For it was here that the creators had flocked and taken hiding after the National Uprising; it was here that I could best serve my country and protect the people from these terrorists. I hoped that the reason The Chief was calling his first and second detective, Kenneth and me, into his office that day was to assign us a case that had to do with the rumor among the officers that the creators were rising again. If that were so, it would be the biggest case I had ever taken on, and if I could show that it was me—and not Kenneth—who solved it, then The Chief would have no choice but to consider me for a promotion to First Detective.

Two beggars began to follow me. I could hear their footsteps, feel their stares on my back, smell their filth. I stopped walking and turned around. One of them had a face covered with a black bushy beard and wasn't wearing any shoes. The other had his shirt off and his rib cage was poking out of his skin. His eyes were melancholy, and a startlingly sharp lime green.

They came closer but not *too* close. Then the beggar with the green eyes spoke.

"You 'ave water? There's none 'ere. We're dyin.'" He looked me up and down. "And I can tell you're a kind man."

They'd make up anything to fill their bellies.

"I don't have any food or water," I responded. "I am sorry."

I turned around, without looking at their pleading faces. But as I continued walking, I could hear their footsteps behind me. I turned back around, more forcefully this time, reached into the inside right pocket of my ash-gray nanojacket, and took out my wave gun, which shot blue-purple waves with a soft murmur and could burn a man's skin. The bearded beggar squealed and ran away. But the other one stood his ground.

"I 'aven't eatin' or had enough water in months. Please help."

Tightening my lips and swallowing hard, I shook my head.

He stared into me, shooting arrows with his sharp eyes. Then he approached, and got too close.

I aimed my wave gun at his chest.

"Don't make me shoot you."

"Okay, okay," he replied, putting up his hands.

"Good luck," I muttered. Though the beggars backed off, I could feel them watching me as I walked on, wondering why I had come this way. I swore to myself I would take the skytrain the next time I went to the station like other people of my class, or even the airpath. I didn't want to cause any trouble. But I told myself the same thing the last time I walked through the Slums. What was it that drew me to this place? Even the color of the dirt seemed to match my coffee-colored eyes and brown hair in a strange, familiar way.

The other officers thought I took the weekly journey because I was trying to act tough, to show off, and to impress The Chief. I was the only person on the force who was an Upperclassman, due to my wife, which perplexed the other officers even more. Kenneth once said, in what I perceived as an envious tone, that I walked through the Slums precisely *because* I was an Upperclassman. What he was implying was that I did it out of guilt. Or maybe it was that although I felt safer on the skytrain and in my car, then I was the same—like everybody else. The Slums were repulsive, the beggars dangerous, but it was *different*, and there was my childhood yearning to see the outside world— something, *anything* different. It was on that day— when the beggar approached me, and then what happened next—that I consciously realized that there was something I longed for, a missing piece, though I didn't know what that was at the time. All I knew was that there was a void in my life that I desperately needed to fill.

Soon after the beggar backed away, I spotted the police station. It was like an oasis in the middle of a desert. It was originally built here so we could keep an eye on the beggars. I could spot the Doric columns that lined the entrance and the ten white marble steps that led inside. As quickly as the rain began, it stopped, and a heavy sun took over the sky. I adjusted my nanojacket from "off" to "cool" and almost tripped over the head of a beggar. When I looked up, I could see a man leaning on one of the columns. It was Kenneth.

First Detective Kenneth Fletcher had black, parted hair, shifty brown eyes, and a bulging, cleft chin. Beneath his exterior was a wild temper, held tightly in his chest, which like a ticking bomb could explode at any minute. But mostly, I couldn't think of Kenneth without imagining his strained, sly smile. Kenneth never opened his mouth when he smiled, as if he were hiding his opinion of you between his teeth.

I was only Second Detective, and wouldn't get my badge until the First Detective retired. But it was me who solved our last case, a terrorist plot at a bank, and Kenneth who nearly screwed it up. I uncovered the bomb wrapped to the man's chest, but before I did, Kenneth went trigger-happy and accidentally shot an officer in the Technological Police Force. It was a reckless blunder; there was no mistaking the TPF, completely dressed in black with goggles that covered half their faces and belts that held every weapon imaginable. With their direct connection to President Lapin, I was sure Kenneth's career working for The City Police would be over if The Chief knew what had happened. But no one actually witnessed Kenneth kill that officer. No one but me.

When Kenneth heard me approach, only his eyes moved to size me up under lowered lids. He wasn't smiling then and I knew why. I knew what he wanted.

"Do you remember what we talked about?" he asked. "You're gonna back me up? Say I shot that officer in self—"

Kenneth, seeing something in the corner of his eye, whipped out his wave gun and shot it down the steps, the low murmur of the gun reverberating around me. It was the beggar with the green eyes. He flailed his arm up and down, the blue-purple waves infiltrating his skin.

"He'll have a nasty burn later," Kenneth remarked. As he held his wave gun by his side I could see, poking through his nanojacket, the front of his liquidator.

The short squirting noise liquidators make as they release their rapid stream of water lasts less than the time you can snap your fingers. But in that instant, the force and jolting speed of the water makes certain that with a direct hit, it could kill.

"You didn't have to do that."

"I know, Vic, you think you can control 'em with your mind. But it's a detective's job to protect the people against filth. Get that through your head. Well? What was it we talked about?"

"It was in self-defense."

"That's right," he said, and smiled, that damned strained smile, and patted me on the back. "That's my boy," he remarked, though I was only ten years younger than him. "You'll be a great First Detective some day."

"It could be sooner than 'some day' if you ever retire!" I said, laughing, while watching him through half-shut eyes.

"Retire?" He gave a loud snort. "From First Detective? I'd be a fool to do so. Besides, you know I get a bonus for my next case. And with that money, I can finally pay off those house loans and get Dora off my ass ..." his voice trailed off and his eyes looked up at the sky. Kenneth poured his energy into his work, and I knew it was all for his wife. He cleared his throat with one sharp cough and straightened his posture, his reflective gaze turning into a piercing stare. He was looking down the steps, the sound of running feet entering our ears. It was the beggar again. He wouldn't give up. He was racing toward me.

"Please!" he shouted. "You must 'ave a drop of water!"

He bound up the fifth step, the fourth, the third…

"You gonna shoot him?" Kenneth asked.

He leaped over the second step, to the first, and I could smell his heavy breath, see the desperation in his eyes—

Kenneth took out his liquidator and shot the beggar in the face. The sound of the squirt, the rushing water, the helpless beggar falling down the steps …. it's a moment etched in my mind. Blood spurted out of his head, the same color as mine, its stench permeating the air.

"That's what he gets for coming into the station," Kenneth said. He glared at me with disgust. "What has gotten into you?"

The bearded beggar came running toward the man, falling over bodies, his mouth open, his face distorted. "My brother!" he shouted as he reached the man and crouched down beside him. When he shouted those words, I thought back to *my* brother, remembering what happened to him.

"Let's go," Kenneth said and we walked into the station. But I looked back, and when I did, the beggar stared into my eyes. I could feel him peering into my soul, and I wanted to reach out my arm to him, take his dirt-encrusted hand, and lead him out of this place, to the sky, or the setting sun. But it was too late. I followed Kenneth, rays of light dancing on his badge, into the station, and away from a world where I felt strangely compelled to return.

Chapter Two: The Case

The Chief had a mustache that moved while he talked. He combed it regularly. It was sharp, pencil thin, and as expressive as a man's eyebrows. He kept an electric razor in his front pocket, which he would use in front of the mirror before important meetings. His office shelves held an impressive collection of razors of all kinds: from the microscopic that could pluck away at the root of the smallest hairs, to the wide and exotic, which could give a man a perfect shave in a single stroke. Although he was sixty-five, he looked much younger. "Appearance is success," he was known to say.

On this particular morning, The Chief's mustache looked thinner than usual. This meant The Chief had a rather long trimming session, probably indicating a heightened state of anxiety. He was rummaging through the top drawer of his wide desk as Kenneth and I came in. When he saw us, he shoved the drawer shut, and instructed in his smoke-stained voice, "Sit down, the both of you." We sat in two shaky wooden chairs across from his desk. I could see myself behind that desk, assigning cases to younger detectives. The Chief only wore his badge on special occasions, and I found myself wondering if he kept it somewhere in that drawer he had so quickly closed.

"Well?" The Chief asked, his lip curling upward, his eyes on Kenneth, "You have a lot of explaining to do. What happened at the bank?"

"The fucker shot at me. What was I supposed to do? It was in self-defense, Chief."

"Is that true, Victor?"

I looked behind The Chief at the giant portrait next to his collection of razors. It was of Detective Conrad, my hero. He was the greatest detective the department had ever known, who always said it was an officer's job, first and foremost, to protect the people.

I had given my partner my word. He had taken me under his wing for the past ten years. Taught me how to be a detective. Kenneth was a dutiful officer of the law and loyal to The Nation. I respected him for that. I also knew that he loved his wife more than anything, and that they were going through difficult times, and that with the bonus he'd earn by taking on the next case, he'd have enough money to pay off the loans on his house, and relieve his wife's worst financial fears.

But Detective Conrad did what was right … and Kenneth was cruel to anyone who got in his way. He treated beggars as if they were subhuman. Ultimately, we had different philosophies. And I was sick and tired of covering up for him. Plus … truth be told, I wanted that badge.

So I said it.

"Detective Fletcher went wild, Chief, firing rounds with his liquidator. One of the bullets hit the TPF officer. Sorry, Kenneth, but I can't lie for you anymore. A policeman's duty is to protect the people."

Kenneth turned his head slowly and gave me an incredulous glare of contempt. "After all I did for you, you betray me like this?"

"You could have killed *me*, the way you were

10

shooting!"

"The fact is, Kenneth," The Chief interrupted, "it doesn't matter. The TPF will be after you. And they'll be after *me* too and the department unless we do something."

"I have a friend in the TPF," Kenneth tried to explain. "With more clout than the man I shot. He'll back me up."

"Look," said The Chief, clearing his throat. "In recent years, you've become trigger happy. No one knows about the beggars you killed—but a TPF officer? Sure, you have a friend in the TPF, and maybe you can get away with this, and I hope for your sake you do, but I can't put this burden on the department. So I'm asking that you seek an early retirement. Relax and spend some time with your wife and daughter. Victor, I'm promoting you to First Detective."

I could hardly believe my ears. This was it—the moment I had been waiting for! I was going to pin the badge on the front of my nanojacket. I could see my wife smiling as I placed it in her hands, and my son with a proud twinkle in his eye. Then I had a strange thought. If this was what I was working for, and I had gotten it at the age of thirty-four, then what? A heaviness weighed down on my eyes.

Kenneth shot out of his seat. "This is *bullshit!*" he flipped. "It was in self-defense, I tell you, what was I supposed to do?"

"You shot the wrong man," said The Chief, his gruff voice unwavering. "I have no choice."

"And my...bonus?"

"Only with one more case, Kenneth."

Kenneth stood there for a second, motionless, his face inches from The Chief's, his shifty brown eyes peering into The Chief's large, dark irises. Then he opened his mouth, and spit in The Chief's face. He turned to me, and with a piercing stare, he said, "You'll regret this, Victor Vale." Then he stormed out, slamming the door shut.

The Chief wiped the spit off his cheek with a tissue. "Those detectives with a wild side, they never last. That's why there's hope for you, Victor. You've got a good head on your shoulders."

"Thanks, Chief." He put his hands on his desk and I followed them with my eyes, seeing if they'd open that drawer and take out the badge.

"You're sort of old school, but it works for you. Walking through the Slums like you own the place. I like that. But I'm not going to make you First Detective yet … officially. I have a case for you and I want to see how you do with it. I believe you're the man for this case but you'll have to prove that yourself. Then I'll consider giving you your badge."

So I wasn't getting the badge after all. Yet. The heaviness on my eyes was gone and I found myself leaning forward, looking directly at The Chief.

"I'll solve whatever case you've got for me. But if I'm going to take it without a First Detective's salary then I want your signature, *in type*, that I'll get the detective's badge after I solve it."

The Chief chuckled. His protruding belly shook up and down as he laughed and his garlic breath reached across the desk and smacked me in the face. "Who do you think you are? Your hero, Detective Conrad? We didn't even grant that sort of treatment to him. Why are you so special?"

"You said it yourself. You *need* me on this case. I think that's part of the reason you fired Kenneth. Now I can't be sure what the case is, but I have the notion that it involves … creators."

"How would you know that?"

"You said I was 'old school.' Creators have not conformed like the rest of us so who better than your least conventional detective? You also commented on my walk through the Slums so you know I don't fear beggars, and creators are often beggars. So maybe the case is involving me infiltrating a community of creators, who say, are probably planning some sort of revolt."

The Chief was silent for a moment. "Good, Victor. It looks like you've developed some deductive reasoning skills. Or you've been gossiping with the other officers," he added with a wink.

"But there is more. You seem overly anxious today and a case is just a case. No. This is personal. Ever since the National Uprising, you've wanted revenge against the people who killed Andy. This may very well be your best chance."

The Chief glared at me with his large, dark eyes. The image of The Chief's son bleeding on the steps in front of the station—it … it was in nearly the same spot where Kenneth killed that beggar. I was only three during the National Uprising but for those of you who are old enough, I'm sure you remember it all over the news. The senior officers who were there the day of the Uprising were hesitant to talk about it, but I've managed to fill in the details of how it happened.

The infamous Leo Weinstein and his forces—the beggars and creators—stormed the station. We fought back, shooting our liquidators through open windows and from the satellite-strewn rooftop. Not a single person penetrated the station. The beggars could not move up those white marble steps; they could not defeat the officers, the protectors of the Upper Class. Officers were killed though, the boldest ones pushing apart the tall steel doors behind the Doric columns, picking off Weinstein's men left and right. Some of Weinstein's forces had acquired guns, and seeing an officer's face was enough reason to shoot him. The Chief's son was one of those officers. He was the youngest on the whole force at eighteen years old. The Chief was in his office at the time, taking orders from the TPF. Apparently, he looked out his office window and saw his son being killed—the same image we saw on UNICÉ—and screamed with maniacal horror. I couldn't imagine how The Chief felt when he realized he was too late to save his son. There, on a shelf of its own above the razors, was a small comb that his son had used on the day he died. Over thirty years and The Chief still hadn't touched it. He never talked about his son and I thought that I had gone too far by mentioning his name. I had been too audacious, too direct. When he finally spoke, I could see a redness forming around his irises.

"All right, Victor. I'll give you my signature. But if you mess up this case, you're not getting your detective badge. In fact, you're out altogether. Got it?"

"Got it." I swallowed. What had I done?

The Chief lifted his upper lip, his mustache signaling a change in thought. "Now for the details. We have reason to believe that there is a community of creators meeting at Huppington Books™."

Huppington Books™ was not only the largest publishing company in The Nation but also happened to be my wife's client. That's right, Anji was representing Huppington Books™ and defending the paper book industry in the trial against the environmentalists. If Sylvester Huppington was a creator, then my wife was unknowingly a traitor to The Nation and was risking imprisonment or worse. The less she knew, the better. I

14

had to keep this case from Anji.

I started picking at the leather on the arm of my chair.

"Huppington Books™ is a government financed business," I replied. "Sylvester Huppington is an Upperclassman! He can't be a creator—"

"We got a tip from someone inside. We believe that a resistance movement is brewing there and that this has been the source of the terrorist threats, including the one at the bank. We need you to go undercover. Gain their trust. Pretend to be one of them and find out if they're planning an uprising. We think they have a weapons facility and there's a code to get in. Sylvester Huppington wouldn't reveal it to our other undercover agent, who is now off the case. Get in there. Get some evidence of weapons or bomb making. They will be used in court to prove intent of acts of terrorism against The Nation. Bring that evidence to me, and you've done your job. That's all you need to know. Don't contact me unless I contact you. You won't be returning to the station unless the TPF call you in." His mustache twitched. "This case comes from the top. If it turns out that Huppington really is planning an uprising and we stop them, you and I will be heroes. You know the government will make us set for life. And the department will have all the money and power it'll ever need."

"Why doesn't Lapin take care of this herself though? It still makes no sense. If Lapin thinks that Sylvester Huppington is a creator, why doesn't she kill him and send the TPF to raid the place? Why involve us?"

"I believe she's afraid that if she raids the movement, it will cause a more serious rebellion among the masses."

I found myself gazing at the portrait of Detective Conrad. "I can't imagine what she'd do to us ... if we failed."

"We won't fail!!" The Chief shouted and I tried to ignore his garlicky breath lingering in the air. He was in a fury like I had never seen, the redness in his eyes spreading to tomato-like cheeks. "It's time that the creators met their demise. And I'm depending on you, Detective Vale." He glared into my eyes. "Don't let me down."

"You have my word, Chief. But one last question— why do you want me on such an important case? There are other detectives with a lot more experience. This will be my first case as Detective."

"It's not me who wanted you on this case. It's *President Lapin*. She has an undercover officer in there. Someone who has been there for years now. From the TPF. But Sylvester still won't reveal the code to him. Apparently, she thinks he'll reveal it to you."

"I've never met the man in my whole life."

"Well, he requested to see you."

"He requested to see *me*?"

"Well, not exactly *you*. He requested an exclusive interview with a certain reporter at the People's News … your alias, Walter Cunningham."

Walter Cunningham was my second-half, my alternate persona, the man I pretended to be to protect my identity. He was an accomplished correspondent from the People's News, The City's only celebrity newspaper.

"Why would he do that?"

"If you don't know then I don't know. Regardless, you have to befriend Sylvester—gain his trust. Then have him tell you the code to the weapons facility, or convince him to take you in there. And get that evidence."

Why would Sylvester Huppington request Walter Cunningham for an interview? I'd only seen Sylvester in advertisements where he pontificated about the power of reading, the great accomplishments of The Nation, and the heroic deeds of President Lapin. Of all people, Sylvester would be the last person I'd expect to be a creator—he was the ultimate government pawn, the king of propaganda. But then again, sometimes what you least expect comes true.

Chapter Three: Home

I still remember the days the Spiraling Tower was being built. Automatrons assembled the silo-like core, then took factory-built parts complete with wiring and plumbing, and hauled them up with long, thin cables that looked like arm-like extensions of the automatrons themselves. In this way, each floor was attached to the rotating central axis. From a distance, the tower looked like an ice cream cone swirling into the sky.

On the roof of each story were solar panels, which gathered sunlight at different times of the day depending on the tower's rotation. Between the floors were silent wind turbines, which allowed each floor to turn at its own speed and direction. As I stepped onto the mechanized walkway from the skytrain port toward the triple-decker elevator on the thirty-third floor, I saw yet another inane pigeon fly into the gigantic fans between the thirteenth and fourteenth stories. Its feathers flew at the skin of glass in front of me before floating through the breeze and down to the Slums below.

Although the Spiraling Tower seemed like it was controlled by the powers of nature, it was, of course, also operated by a computer, which was somewhere beneath the sleek, teal marble floor of the ground entrance. The suites spun on command, which Anji and I used most often to watch both sunrises and sunsets from our bedroom window. Each suite had its own lift, which brought your car from one of the bottom seventeen floors of the parking garage directly to your door. Unlike most residents, who owned cars but made little use of them, I used my vehicle on cases, changing its color and design to suit my purpose.

As I stepped into the maroon carpeted elevator and told it to take me to the eighty-sixth floor, I thought about that car. I had been waking up in the middle of the night with strange inclinations to drive through the Slums, imagining myself rolling down the windows, listening to the violent shouts and helpless whimpers, taking in the smell of feces and decay, staring ahead into the dark abyss. But then I would hear Anji's peaceful snores, and I'd eventually fall back asleep.

I stepped out of the elevator and onto the walkway to my home: apartment 868. "Open!" I commanded, and with a click, the door unlocked. I went straight to my office. It was the room in my house where I felt the freest, where I could be alone, investigate cases, play cubes, and download knowledge.

An oval, spotless window was situated above my crimson desk so that light would seep into the room as I worked. The metal walls of my office were sleek silver. There were two framed pictures on the edge of my desk: one of my wife, with two chestnut curls outlining her soft face, and one of my son, with a slight, wry smile, and a blockball cap.

Detective Conrad was my hero and I couldn't resist entering Virtual World to *become* him. I motioned my hand to the top drawer. It opened and I took out my glasses and nanokit. I put on the glasses and from the kit, I took out a vile, syringe, and a smooth case the size of a coin. I carefully removed a nanotron from the case with two fingers and inserted it into the vile. I then poked the tip of the syringe into the vile and watched as the miniscule computer was drawn into it. I stuck the needle into my upper arm. I hit a vein. In an instant, I sensed the computer working in my brain. I could feel the RAM shooting through my arms and legs, storing itself within the nuclei and mitochondria of my body's cells. I waited a moment for the funny feeling to cease before entering Virtual World. Then I allowed myself to *transform*. To become Detective Conrad, the greatest detective this city has ever known.

I *was* my hero. I wanted to *become* him on the day he retired from the force. I attempted to create the world I desired. Through his eyes, I saw a road, purple rays of sun reflecting on the blacktop. The monotonous voice of the nanotron computer spoke of the man I had *become*, "Detective Conrad, the famous, enigmatic detective, has retired today. He was an officer of the law who was committed to upholding his duty as a policeman, and was always loyal to his country. We thank you, Detective, and will miss you, for your service to the citizens of The Nation."

I listened through his ears. To the awed voices speaking 'thank yous.' Watched people's faces as I passed. Children's gazes, men and women tipping their hats. Their heads nodding, a pair of eyes looking into mine and then down, where the badge I had worn for thirty years was pinned securely to my front pocket. I nodded back at them, humbly, and went on my way, down the road, as I allowed myself to smile, knowing I had done right, and Detective Conrad's image, *my* image, slowly faded into the purple sun …

… my head felt light, my mind confused, as I walked into the dark void, as if I was entering a cave. In only a few seconds, the trip was over, I left the dreamlike state where I was everything I wished for, drifting out of Virtual World … to other corners of UNICÉ.

Yabble© dictionary defines UNICÉ [yü-ni-sey] (Universal Network of Intelligent Conscious Entities), a term coined by a famous futurist long ago, as:

1) a self-aware cosmic consciousness;
2) the collective consciousness of man, the interpenetration of computers, and the Internet;
3) cyberspace.

Well, there certainly weren't a shortage of advertisements. As I *transformed* back into Victor Vale, reaching out my arms, tearing open the darkness like curtains, I stepped into a cloudy sky and images emerged from the puffy clouds of the UNICÉ message room: a bottle of Elena™ Perfume spraying its sweet nectarine scent into the air, a sexy low voice suggesting, "a gift for your wife." A pair of Kelly Karr Variety Footwear™ kicking into the air, a man insisting, "why not get your lady the newest brand of moldable shoes?"; an arctic cola, bits of ice-cold water dripping down the metal can, a woman whispering, "simply refreshing … treat yourself." I closed my eyes and the images faded as I spoke:

"Messages."

"No messages," replied the computer in its automated voice.

I looked into the sky and uttered, "News." A soft, maroon chair materialized beside me. I sat as the newsman's bald head appeared in the clouds, his monotonous voice resounding in the cool breeze that comforted my cheeks. His expressions were mechanical, his voice robotic, his emotions unwavering, as he spoke, "Headline story. Terrorists attacked a bank, fully armed and carrying bombs. The Technological Police Force was able to defuse the bombs and no civilians were injured. Tragically, one TPF officer was killed."

By Kenneth. But what did the public know? I asked, "Who killed the TPF officer?"

"One of the terrorists," the newsman replied.

"Were there any City Police officers at the scene? Was there a mention of a man by the name of Detective Kenneth Fletcher?"

"You have asked too many questions," the newsman said, his face still. "You will receive a logic bomb if you ask another."

"Do NOT send any logic bombs, botnets, or firewalls. I'm a detective. Goodbye."

"Good day ..." the newsman said, his head fading into a cloud of white.

"Return," I spoke into the air, and my image dissolved like a sugar cube in a glass of water. The twinge of warmness shot through me as I came back into my body, sitting at my office desk. I slowly removed the syringe from my upper arm and wiped its tip with a white piece of cloth. I tapped a finger on the bridge of my glasses and a small lever popped open. I carefully placed a nanotron inside. Somehow or another, I needed access to UNICÉ at all times.

I wanted to watch the sunset. So I walked out of my office and through the hall to our balcony. In the summer, Anji liked to garden here. She planted tomatoes, cucumbers, basil, rosemary, and gotu kola. These vegetables and herbs were plotted in the center of the balcony while forget-me-nots gave off notions of tranquility and lilacs exuded a scent of innocence as you stepped outside onto the soft, welcoming, forest green turf. A stream flowed counterclockwise, reaching all four corners of the balcony in a symmetrical square of surrounding water. It was all wonderfully fake, from the hand-painted basil to the perfume-scented lilacs.

I looked out at The City through the external glass skin that protected our garden from the darkened mist accumulated from years of pollution. The blinking white light of the Guardian, that grand satellite, was above, soaring through the clouds, protecting us from harm. It comforted me to know that no nation could attack us; we controlled the sky. I could see the Statue of Lapin, make out the reflections of sunlight melting the silver stone, and could spot The City Bridge in the distance. When night fell, all I could see were the nearest skyscrapers: the Dancing Towers, the Water Pyramid, and the tallest building of all, The Mountain, with its massive structure dwarfing the others. From the skytrain, the air was clear, but never this high. The trickling of the stream in my ears, I found myself staring into a foggy, polluted haze until the clouds turned black and I could just make out the tiny lights of The City through the smog. I didn't know why I bothered looking for the setting sun.

I walked through the hall to my wife's office. "Open!" I said to her door, but it didn't budge.

"Just a minute!" Anji exclaimed.

I wondered what she was locking her door for when it opened with a click. The walls of Anji's office were covered with diplomas and pictures. There was the photo of Anji and I drinking wine on one of our first dates and a picture of an eight-year-old Tommy stirring a cup of chocolate milk. But one photo she placed directly behind her desk. It was of her father. I might as well tell you now—her father was the famous lawyer, Dallas Grumm. His arms were folded in that picture, and he wore a suit and tie, just as distinguished as you would have imagined. He was standing in front of The City Courthouse, his chin raised and his eyes with a look of confidence mixed with satisfaction. As I entered the room, I looked from the painting to Anji and my lips tightened, never forgetting it was a long way to measure up.

Anji was pushing her desk drawer shut, causing her Holographic Teleportation Device (HTD), the black specimen that could fit in the palm of her hand, and a full glass of water, to shake. Anji turned her face from the orange light that shone from the HTD, and looked at me with tired eyes, strands of hair falling against her cheek. The first time I met my wife those eyes mesmerized me. Their caramel color, the way she batted them at me when I talked about my job, that wild look in moments of passion, how when she laughed they disappeared behind her eyelids. But those eyes had begun to look tired since she took on the trial against the Environmentalists, as if she had been in the heat of a battle. And usually, she was.

"What were you doing?" I asked.

"Oh, don't get me started," she said, turning off the HTD.

"What did you need to lock the door for?"

"They tried to make a settlement. But there was no way I'd let them do that. We're going to trial. It's the only way Dad would have wanted it."

"Do *you* want it?"

"Of course I do," she replied sharply. "More than anything."

I knew how much this trial meant to Anji. But I really wished she wouldn't stress so much about it. The last time she lost a trial, I found her on the floor of her office, hardly breathing. Who knows what would have happened if I hadn't seen her and brought her salbutamol jacket. Looking at her lying there, struggling to breathe, crying, as if she were drowning in a sea of disappointment—it scared the shit outta me. Anji's asthma had been acting up since her father passed away a year and a half ago, and she was taking her work more seriously than ever. Although you may think of Dallas Grumm as the triumphant, abundantly rich, controversial corporate lawyer, he was a demanding and uncompromising man who Anji tried to escape from by marrying me at the age of twenty-one. Yet Anji loved and respected the success that her father had earned. When he died, passing the law firm into her hands, she became determined to carry on his legacy. It was in his shadow that I lived.

"Just try not to stress too much about it, honey," I said. "Besides, I have good news. I've been made First Detective."

Her eyes lit up. "Oh, Victor!" She jumped out of her seat and wrapped her arms around my waist. I kissed her. "Can I see your badge?"

"I don't get it until I solve one more case. But I'll solve it."

"I know you will." She gazed longingly into my eyes. "I'm so happy."

A door creaked shut down the hall.

"Is Tommy studying?" Anji asked. "The seventh grade examinations are slowly approaching and you know that after this year it will be time to set up his pension plan. Every time I go check on him, his door is locked and it takes him a good five minutes to open it. I hear him shuffling around, drawers opening and closing, but he insists that he's preparing for his exams … I think he's up to something." She hesitated before asking, "Do you think Tommy is truly committed to taking over his grandfather's firm?" She gazed out the window at the sky, as if trying to will something to come out of the clouds and tell her the future.

"Yes," I said, surprised that she'd even ask. "All the boy has ever talked about since he was five years old was how he wanted to be a lawyer. He knows what we expect of him."

She gave me a quick, skeptical glance. But then she smiled. "You're right. Wanna eat?"

"Has Henry gone shopping alrea—?" I started to ask when the loud buzz of the doorbell shot through the house and into my ears.

"Here it is now. BRB!" Anji slid her arms off me and walked out of the room. I watched her go, wondering why she still used so many abbreviations. She click-clacked down the hallway in her Kelly Karr Moldable Shoes™. I found it sexy when she wore her platform pumps that could change shape around her toes and had adjustable heels that could rise up to two feet high (though Anji rarely wore them over ten inches except in court). She opened the front door as our automatron was getting out of the car. When we first got Henry, Tommy thought he was human. I supposed he looked like an Upperclassman, with his collared shirt, khaki pants, and polished shoes. Except of course for his black metal, which Tommy mistook for skin.

Henry took out two shopping bags and went into the kitchen. I sat in my chair at the head of the round table while the automatron put the food in the refrigerator and cabinets. Anji instructed him to take out three hamburgers, which he put in the zapster for two seconds, and then plopped on three plates.

"They're from McDougal's™ Lab, the best modifier in The City," Anji said to no one in particular. She looked at Henry. "Isn't that right?"

"Yes, Mrs. Vale. McDougal's™ hamburgers are the best on the planet."

"Bring Tommy his dinner."

Henry did a quick pivot and turned on his heels 180 degrees. Then he marched, one foot in front of the other, down the hall to Tommy's room.

"Do you really think Tommy needs to eat in his room again?" I asked.

"Yes, dear, until his exams are finished."

Henry turned, pivoting 180 degrees on his heels, and marched, one foot in front of the other, back down the hallway and into the kitchen.

"Thank you, Henry," Anji said as the door to Tommy's room shut.

"May I go recharge now?"

"Yes. See you in the morning." Henry left the apartment to the recharge room as Anji sat at the kitchen table, setting her glasses down beside her dish. "Well?" she asked me. "Tell me about your first case."

I was hoping she wouldn't ask. Anji and I were open to each other about work. It was such a big part of our lives. We both *believed* in our work and in the importance of career. Everyone did, of course. Yet for us, it was more; it was a way we connected. But I still couldn't tell Anji about it. The less she knew, the less chance she'd be implicated, if God forbid it ever came to that.

"Can't tell you, babe. It's for your own safety. Sorry, but this is the only way."

She looked down at her plate, and said, "I understand." Then she lifted her glasses to her face.

We ate. As we reached for our burgers and put them to our mouths, our eyes darted back and forth, using the nanotrons in our brains to explore UNICÉ. While Anji was reading her favorite celebrity magazines, I was on the Yabble© encyclopedia, examining Sylvester Huppington's bio, its pages illuminated on the back

28

of my retinas. I was glad the technocrats who worked with President Lapin hadn't yet invented a way to share visions on UNICÉ from one set of eyes to another; I was always able to do private research at the dinner table. Of course there were hackers who could penetrate the system, but the penalty was hardly worth the crime.

Hacking into the Detective Database could cost you two years in prison. But that was nothing. Did you know that the punishment for hacking into a government network was forty years in a penitentiary? That's four times the sentence for eyeglass theft. Can there be an adequate punishment for hacking into another person's brain? I suppose when the Internet was invented years ago, and became more and more a central part of people's lives, until it became essential to their being, ingrained within their *heads*, it was inevitable that it would come to this. How do we draw the line between the cyber world and what we know as reality? When do those two worlds become one and the same?

These thoughts went through my head until I focused my eyes and brain on Huppington's bio. He had such an illustrious career. Rumor had it that he met the President herself. I was still shocked that the most renowned publisher and a man so loyal to The Nation was a creator.

"Did you know that Kelly Karr has a new boyfriend?" Anji asked.

I didn't hear her. We sat there, reaching our hands to our mouths, taking slow bites without realizing the juicy, meaty taste, putting the burger onto the plate so we could digest, and then lifting it again, moving our arms as mechanically as the automatrons. Every now and then, Anji and I would throw a comment into the air, but our words seemed to linger in the empty space.

We only half-listened.

"Kelly Karr's in a new movie called Hollywood Hearts. She meets someone in virtual world and then later, she sees him on the skytrain, and well, you can guess the ending."

A few months after Anji and I started dating in college, she said she wanted to take acting classes. There was a light that shone in her eyes when she said that. When I told her she was as pretty as any movie star, she smiled shyly and her face turned red, which rarely happens anymore. It wasn't my compliment that made her blush though. "Is that your dream? To be a star?" I asked, taking her hand. "You'll always be *my* star." I'd say anything to get her to smile and bat those eyes at me.

Later that week, her father came to visit. I knew I had to introduce myself to the famous Dallas Grumm, and although I was intimidated, I was resolved to speak to him that day. But when I went to her room and heard her father's commanding voice for the first time, I knew it wasn't the right moment. His voice beamed through the door, "No daughter of mine will be an actress." "Yes, Dad," was all Anji said in response. I tried to comfort her when I had her alone, but nothing I could say would make her feel any better. I told her I believed in her and that she could do anything she set her mind to. But to my shock, that only made her more upset. "No," she said, "My father is right." Anji could fight in a courtroom against the most powerful men in The City and win, but when it came to standing up to her father, she melted like a little girl.

I took off my glasses. "Can we stop using our nanotrons?"

"I know this celebrity stuff is silly, honey. It's just a nice esca—"

"It's not that. It's that every dinner, we sit around, downloading information, but we don't actually talk to each other."

"Oh." Anji took off her glasses. "What was it you wanted to talk about?"

"I just thought we'd talk."

"Okay...what about?"

I hesitated. Did I really want to get into this? There was no way she would understand. But then again— what if she somehow did?

"Do you ever think … of giving back? I mean, we have so much. Do you ever think of giving … to the *beggars*?"

"The beggars!" Anji exclaimed with a look of surprise. "Don't you remember how they killed Upperclassmen in the National Uprising? The news reports said that most likely beggars are behind the recent terrorist attacks. Even *you* said you thought the bomb in the bank was planted by beggars!"

"And I still think that, but … the motto of the police has always been that we have a duty to serve and protect the people. It doesn't say 'Upperclassmen!'"

"Times have changed since The Purge. I've worked hard. Why should I give away what I've earned?"

"You know as much as me how impossible it is for them to move up in class, even if they work hard. Maybe it's our duty to share what we earn—"

"What *we* earn? Not *you*. My father worked long and hard to support his children!" Her little nose was getting red, which happened when she got upset. I used to think that was kind of cute. I didn't then. "I know that as a policeman you've had a lot of bad experiences with beggars, and I know you've seen many horrible things." She rubbed the top of my hand. "You're so brave." Then she put her hand to her side and looked

31

down at her plate. "But society is what it is, Dad always said. 'In this country, we believe in freedom of choice. The Upper Class dogma is that people choose their own destinies.' We've been given our lot in life, Victor—a fortunate one. So let's try to appreciate what we have."

Always quoting *Dad*. She was right though. I had a beautiful wife, a good son, a job I loved and excelled at, all the money a man could want. Why couldn't I appreciate it? There was no reason for me to be unhappy or unsatisfied. Despite all the information I could learn, all the cases I could solve, all the things I could buy, there was something beneath the nanotrons in the crevices of my brain that I couldn't quite shake off. What I saw in the Slums that day, the death of that beggar in front of his brother, his blood spurting out of his head, the same color as an Upperclassman—it was the first time since I was a child that I began to question things.

No. There was nothing to question. We lived in a great nation. My job was to protect the people. With this new case, I would do just that. And in the end, I'd get my badge.

❦

Anji made sure the bedroom doors were closed at night. She often checked underneath the bed to see if a shoe had found a home there. She didn't like anything to interrupt the flow of her Qi. Our bed was covered with satin sheets. It faced the door and we each had an identical square-shaped, apricot-colored bedside table, which Anji had picked out from the Great Mall. The walls were a light shade of peach, the color Anji had wanted, and the fruity scent of the room came from

Anji's light sprays of perfume. A skin of glass that overlooked The City stretched from the door to Anji's side of the bed. On the other side of the room were our closets and Anji's table, with her large brush, a mirror, and a box of jewelry.

Anji's closet was nearly half the size of our bedroom, and it was mainly occupied with shoes. Boxes lined the shelves with labels, "Peep Toe Pumps with Bow Accents," "Suede Brown for Work," "Strappy Sandals White Summer Triangular," etc., etc. There were also hats, scarves, dresses, jewelry—you name it. There was even one of her father's old kimonos. Anji rarely used anything in there besides the clothes that rested on a gold bar, which shot out of the wall at the sound of her voice. These clothes I was most familiar with: her suits and ties for work, the dresses she wore out for dinner or to go see a movie at the Sky Theater on the top of The Mountain (occasions that rarely happened anymore because we were so busy working), her salbutamol jacket, her sex gown, her pink sleepsuit, and, of course, on a ledge that stuck out an inch from the floor, more pairs of shoes.

My closet was small and I liked it that way. All I kept in there were my clothes, a toolkit, and a blockball bat, which I homered with in the final game during my senior year of high school. When I saw it leaning against the closet wall, I often thought back to that game, the way I tightened my grip around the bat's wooden handle and rested the rectangular barrel on my shoulder in the batter's box, how I swung and connected, the ball sailing through the air; nothing mattered then but the sound of the ball hitting the bat. I'm not one for nostalgia though. I thought I could sell it for a pretty penny; it was made out of wood, after all, long before the tree shortage. Or who knows, maybe

Tommy could make use of it some day.

I was in bed when Anji came into the room and went to her closet. I could feel her glances. She turned so her back faced me and took off her clothes. She slipped on her rosy-red sex gown and then turned to me, giving a naughty smile. I went to my closet and pulled out my navy-blue sex suit. Just seeing it hanging in the closet excited me. When I put it on, I always wanted Anji, and she wanted me.

I stood in front of her. I could feel the hormones being released from her gown into me, and so I threw her on the bed and we went at it, like animals that just understood lust, not love. As I rose to the occasion, came inside of her and she screamed—I felt suddenly dejected, alone. I had forgotten what it felt like to make love.

Chapter Four: Tommy

I used to leave the water running when I brushed my teeth. But since that beggar told me about the lack of water in the Slums, I tightened each faucet of every sink all the way. So when Tommy neglected to turn off the water in our kitchen sink on his way to school the next morning, I decided it was time to teach my son a lesson of my own.

I went into Tommy's room. As a toddler, Tommy loved to tell his room to spin, and he'd chase after his shadow, reflected on the white walls, and then keel over in exuberant exhaustion. After entering kindergarten, Tommy hardly ever used the spin function anymore. It was then that he developed an incredible drive to *succeed*.

As I entered the room, the Holographic Teleportation Device was projecting its rays of light on Tommy, small particles lingering in the orange glow. His body sat at his desk, his lips moving, an arm raised as if he wanted to answer a question. I was waiting for the day we could teleport from place to place in flesh rather than as holographic images, unable to lift an object or feel any physical sensations, yet still experiencing thoughts and emotions. Until then, I had to endure the uncomfortable twinge of warmness you feel when you transmit, so I shut my eyes as I stood in the light from the HTD and transmitted to Tommy's classroom.

My image was standing in the corner of the room, viewing a chaotic mess. The students were either lost on UNICÉ, or out of their seats completely, standing between desks, chatting. A boy and a girl took turns jumping through each other, giving a little shudder, and then jumping again. The teacher was struggling to get their attention. They didn't even notice me. The only eyes that met mine were those of President Lapin, large, somber, and the color of charcoal, in a large photograph that hung above the teacher's desk. There were three-dimensional images of famous figures that lined the walls, all of which were Upperclassmen. The students of Riverton Preparatory School could look up at these men and women and aspire to be like one of them.

There was a large poster board on Tommy's desk. Tommy was still shorter than most of his other classmates, and his blond bangs swung across his forehead when he spoke. Tommy's hair was as thick and as full as his mother's, but with Anji's chestnut curls and my peanut butter brown strands, I often wondered where Tommy got that yellow hue.

"One voice," Ms. Hiccup said. "Be quiiiiiiet!!" she screamed.

The class got quiet. "Thank you," she said with a deep breath. "We have time for one more student to share their report on a famous public figure. Tommy?"

"Yes, but—" Tommy began to say. "I didn't write a report … I drew a portrait."

A portrait? I didn't know Tommy had any sort of interest in drawing. My mind flashed back to my own childhood. I tried not to remember.

"You drew a …" Ms. Hiccup seemed at a loss for a moment. "Oh yes, I did say a portrait was an option, didn't I? But class, remember that you can't draw anything but portraits or paintings of Lapin that are commissioned by The Nation. Anything else is *illegal*. It is only for assignments like these that you can draw, in case a portraitist is the profession you choose to pursue. Okay, Tommy, go ahead."

Thank God Ms. Hiccup made that clear. There were the portraitists, of course, who followed the President and painted her whenever she desired. But what kind of life was that? You were doing a good service to The Nation, but you never made much money.

"Could you pick it up?" Tommy asked, looking at the poster board resting on his desk.

"Ugh, why does everyone always come as a hologram … ?" Ms. Hiccup muttered as she stepped over a backpack on the way to Tommy's desk to lift up the portrait.

"This is a member of my family. My grandpa." Of course. It's always about grandpa. "Some of you may have heard of him."

"Yeah, from *you*," said a boy across the aisle, rolling his eyes. "Since *kindergarten*."

"Why don't you mind your own business, Charlie," Tommy said, staring the kid down. I was proud of Tommy then—standing up for himself. Charlie had spiky hair, high cheekbones, and a body that looked unnaturally strong for a thirteen-year-old boy. You could tell that he had put a lot of effort into his hair that morning; each spike had been molded to perfection with a handful of grease.

Tommy eyed Charlie for another moment before looking back at his portrait. "As I was *saying*, some of you may have heard of Dallas Grumm. He was a famous lawyer who represented many top corporations."

I wished it were me he was talking about. But the

important thing was that the boy's head was in the right place. He'd make more money as a lawyer than a detective.

"My mother is now the head lawyer of my grandpa's firm," Tommy went on. "And I'm going to be a lawyer too and will be as famous as him. But he wasn't just famous," Tommy said with a finger in the air. "My grandpa made enough money to provide for his family. If it weren't for him, I could be living on the street. I want to make a lot of money too so I can marry a beautiful wife like my grandma and have a son and then I'll give him 'Richard Pellman: Virtual Fight 12.'"

"I want 'Virtual Fight 12' but my parents won't give it to me!" Charlie complained to no one in particular.

"I like your portrait," a girl said. She had purple pigtails, freckles scattered around her nose, and dimples on her rosy cheeks. Above one of the dimples was a small bruise.

Tommy's face turned red. "Thanks, Amber," he said.

Back at her desk, Ms. Hiccup illuminated the text of the Gospel of John from her eyeglasses to the board behind her in a font of bold, emerald green. As soon as she turned her back to the class, the students started chatting again.

She whipped back around. "One voice!"

"Ms. Hiiiccup!" Charlie shouted. "My parents told me that only the Gospel of Luke is on the examinations this year. Why do we need to know the Book of John then?"

"Actually, Charlie, both books are on the examinations this year."

The class erupted once again. Students shouted out in protest. The boy and girl went back to jumping through each other. I'd had enough. I came out from the corner and walked down the aisle toward

Tommy's desk.

When the teacher saw me, she let out a great sigh. "Maybe you can help me!" she shouted over the commotion. "What can I do with forty-five holographic students? I can't do show and tell because holograms can't hold anything, I can't offer them candy because they're never hungry. I can't even smack them with a ruler because they wouldn't feel it! If only I were a hologram too, I wouldn't have to commute ten minutes *each way!*"

She chuckled at her inane jokes. I didn't. I turned to face the students. I looked into the eyes of each one to gather their attention and waited for them to be quiet. The girl who was jumping through the boy caught my eye and told the boy to stop. In a matter of seconds, the room had gone silent.

"The Gospel of John is on your examination this year," I said. "I trust Ms. Hiccup." I turned to Tommy. "Because she is the teacher."

"Thank you, Mr. Vale," Ms. Hiccup said. "Now we can proceed with our lesson."

"Thanks, Tommy!" Charlie barked. "If your *dad* didn't show up, we wouldn't have to—"

"Please tell your parents, Charlie," I interrupted, "that students complete the Gospels in the seventh grade."

Charlie scowled at Tommy. "Does your dad fight all your battles for you? I can just learn about this myself, anyway," Charlie muttered. "I'll just download its Yabble© summary page ..." He looked into the lens of his glasses and then read in a mocking voice, 'The Gospel According to John, commonly referred to as The Gospel of John, is an account of the life and ministry of Jesus of Naza—'"

"Charlie Simkis! That's enough!" Ms. Hiccup

scolded. "Get off UNICÉ right now!"

"What's the point? I can learn everything I need on my own."

"I cannot believe," I said, "that this is how a seventh grade class behaves. In my day, we never talked back to our teacher." Charlie rolled his eyes but other students were watching me closely as I spoke.

"Thank you again, Mr. Vale," Ms. Hiccup said.

"It's *Detective* Vale," I replied in a sharp tone. "And this is not what I wanted to see from you either. These kids are completely out of your control." I turned to Tommy. "In your rush to get to class, you left the water running. Don't let it happen again. Although we may have all the water we need, others would do almost anything for a single sip. Let's not squander our resources."

Tommy looked surprised. "Okay, Dad."

"Thank you. See you at dinner. Mom is making your favorite dessert as an early birthday present. Banana oatmeal cookies."

Some of the kids snickered. But Amber, her purple pigtails draped over her shoulders, whispered, "I like those cookies too."

"Okay Dad, now gooo!" Tommy shouted. Before I transmitted back to my office, I saw him glance over at Amber and smile.

Chapter Five: *Huppington Books*

Six hours later, I was no longer Victor Vale. I took out my liquidator, filled it with water, and put on my ash-gray nanojacket, placing my wave gun in the inside right pocket and liquidator in the left. I spoke into the collar, "Bulletproof vest," and I could feel it tightening around my chest. "Activate wound-treaters," I said, and I heard the clicking and snapping around my legs and arms. I took a voice modifier and attached it to the roof of my mouth. I removed a complexion spray can, closed my eyes, and let the cool particles seep into my face, changing my skin to a milky white. I then sprayed my hair so it changed from its natural brown to a yellow hue. I was Walter Cunningham.

I first became Walter Cunningham while on a missing child case at the Academy. I was taking an advanced detective course and we had to solve a real life case in order to pass the class. I didn't really need a disguise but with a voice modifier and complexion spray can at my disposal, I couldn't resist. I went into the bathroom, and while watching my face change in the cracked mirror, I thought of a backstory for Walter Cunningham. He had a happy childhood with parents that loved him and supported his dream to become a reporter. He worked for the Daily News, a celebrity newspaper, not his ideal job, but a job in journalism nonetheless, the profession he desired. He loved green tea and banana pudding.

The case of the missing child was difficult. It wasn't the case itself; in fact, it was a huge success—I discovered the missing boy by following a trail of pretzels. But the moment when the son and father reunited … it reminded me of my own father. I thought I had forgotten the past, put it aside, accepted that I was adopted … that I'd never know my real parents or if I had siblings. But I felt a void deep inside, like a part of me was missing. It was similar to how I felt when I couldn't save the beggar who Kenneth had shot, his brother's eyes staring into mine. It was a feeling that I couldn't push away.

My son once asked if he too could create a disguise. I let him watch me put on my nanojacket, apply the voice modifier, and use the complexion spray. But of course I wouldn't let him get near my closet again. "That was for your eyes only, son, so you could see what I do for a living," I told him after I removed the disguise. "Unless you're a detective like Dad, it's illegal to use any accessories designed for the police. And there mustn't be any illegal activity by a member of this household at any time."

As I tightened my belt, I tried to wrap my head around why Sylvester Huppington requested Walter Cunningham to interview him. But I couldn't think of a reasonable explanation. Well, it certainly made my story easier: Walter, a news reporter, who was requested to interview the great publisher, heard that Sylvester was the leader of an underground lair. A man with clandestine poetic inclinations, Walter goes to the interview with the intention of finding refuge as a creator in Sylvester's movement.

Still, although The Chief told me that Sylvester

Huppington was a creator—the leader of creators!—I wasn't convinced. I needed proof. I had to prove it to myself. I had to take the risk and pretend I wanted to join their movement.

I headed to the portal in my building toward the skytrain that rode to Huppington Books™. I stood beneath the head scanner for half a second as the turquoise ultraviolet lights beamed against my temples, reading the chip in my brain, and the azure-blue letters above flashed: "PAID."

As I stepped onto the skytrain, people rushed to snag a seat, but I stood facing the window. The fasteners wrapped securely around my forearms and calves before the suspended skytrain sped along its track between buildings at lightning speed toward the Round Tower. There was a heavy rain the night before so some of the smog had lifted and the skyscrapers sparkled when the morning sun reflected on them at the right angle. The skytrain sped between towers like a roller coaster, allowing us short glimpses at the electronic billboards that stretched across the buildings. Just below us, the wealthiest commuted to work by flying car or limousine, zooming along the airpath, only to stop at the horizontal traffic lights, which were suspended between buildings by long wires of carbon tubing. Everything around us was as grand and efficient as ever.

No one looked to the streets. The beggars were hungrily searching for scraps left in garbage bins that had been brought downstairs by the automatrons of the Upperclassmen. Only the trees seemed to shout with glee, as the sun shone down on their nourished leaves and satiated trunks.

I was the only person in the skytrain cabin gazing out the window. Although the people there were only a few feet away from me, they seemed distant. Men, women, and children were deep within the crevices of their nanotrons, their pupils darting back and forth, the rest of their faces motionless, except for when they moved their lips to form sounds that only they could hear. They didn't seem to mind when the overbearing nectarine scent of the newest brand of Elena™ perfume leaked into the air from a glowing image of a giant bottle that shone on the face of the Water Pyramid. They didn't seem to notice when we passed by a piercingly loud virtual advertisement on the Dancing Towers; it was for the latest action film where Richard Pellman was shooting his liquidator from one tower to the next, where an alien shrieked, squirmed, and then fell to a lower floor. (Pretty awesome, I know. I saw all his movies.)

I couldn't help becoming amused by the shape of the twenty-five storied Round Tower, which from above resembled that of a large doughnut. As the skytrain dipped downward from its typical height of 500 feet toward the Round Tower, I saw a cluster of apple trees (granny smith, both Tommy's and my favorite kind), lining the back of the building and noticed something peculiar. I activated my Yabble© zoom and focused in to see, nearly hidden from view beneath the leaves of the trees, indented in a clump of mud, a single, rectangular footprint.

Rectangular boots are of the newest variety of Karlton Footwear™ that marketed to Upperclassmen, and as you know, Upperclassmen almost never enter the streets, unless they have some sort of connection to the beggars … or to *creators*. I could make out something silver … was it a steel door handle? I blinked my eyes slowly and deliberately to take a Yabble© photograph of the footprint. As I was storing it as a memory file, the skytrain swung into the doughnut's hole and came to a silent halt. I knew what I would do with that picture.

The fasteners loosened their grip and I stepped out, onto the mechanized walkway that circled the Round Tower. I took the elevator to the fifth floor and when it opened, I was standing in front of the two large royal-purple doors of Huppington Books™. I put my mouth in front of the voice recognition box and said my name.

"Walter Cunningham here." The modifier on the roof of my mouth lowered my voice by two octaves.

"Welcome to Huppington Books™," the monotone high voice of a female automatron emitted through the voice recognition box. "Real or image?"

"Real."

"Come in."

The doors opened slowly, as if they were being pulled by an invisible force on the other side. The ceilings were high and three-dimensional text lined the walls. I could hear the typing of the automatrons at their desks and see the reflection of their hand-sized computers on their black metallic faces. A female automatron sitting at the desk closest to the doors approached me.

"Mr. Huppington is expecting you, Mr. Cunningham. Come this way."

As I followed the automatron through the room, I saw that several of the hand-sized computers were connected with wires.

"Why doesn't he use wireless computers?" I asked the automatron.

"Mr. Huppington uses very old methods."

As we approached Sylvester Huppington's office, I could hear his voice speaking on the phone.

"It'll be just a moment," the secretary said, facing Sylvester's office with her back turned to me. I looked around the room. There were several wires that led into a small compartment in the wall behind one of the automatron's desks. I found myself thinking: could these wires lead to the underground lair? With wires, he couldn't be tracked on UNICÉ. If I went to that compartment, it could cause a commotion, but the automatrons couldn't stop me! What would Kenneth do in this situation? I wanted to resist replicating his reckless nature, but I couldn't help it sometimes; he was, after all, the man who taught me how to be a detective.

So with the secretary's back turned, and the other automatrons immersed in their work, I followed the wires to the wall. The female automatron, sensing my movement, looked back, calling out: "Do not go there!" Soon the other automatrons were shouting these same words almost in unison—"do not go there!"—looking up at me in alarm as I walked past them. I opened the compartment door. The wires inside led through a hole in the floor, and I began to think about why they were there, imagining where they went, picturing veins leading to the heart, noticing the end of one blood-red wire that was sticking dangerously in the air, and as I moved closer to examine it, a hand reached out in front of me—

I heard a perfectly loud scream as the hand turned blue and then purple and the female automatron fell to the floor.

"You didn't have to do that!" I exclaimed, as the other automatrons gathered around.

"Dear me."

I knew that voice. I had grown up listening to Sylvester Huppington announcing the latest books in commercials in that loud and booming voice, which had begun to fade in recent years, and I watched his blond hair turn to a polished silver. It's kind of funny though when you see someone famous face-to-face. There's always something different about them than you had imagined. Seeing Sylvester at that moment, I could make out his tall, bent stature, the wrinkles on his forehead, the crow's feet on the sides of his spectacle-covered eyes. At first, his eyes widened in surprise when he saw what had happened, and then he sighed and shook his head.

"Lucius!" He called to one of the automatrons. "Take Miranda's body, will you? And put it in the incinerator."

And then he looked at me. He gave me the oddest look from the doorway of his office, as if he had just discovered an unusual artifact and was examining it under a microscope. I cleared my throat with a sharp cough. Why was he staring at me like that?

I figured it had to do with the precarious position I was in, squatting on the floor, my head beside an open compartment of wires, and his automatron secretary dead by my side. But I'm not a man to make explanations, which only serve to hint at an ulterior motive, so I stood up, and stared back at Huppington, and asked:

"It's a bit odd to be using wires these days, is it not?"

"They lead to the main computer on the ground floor and I never bothered to get rid of them."

Why didn't he ask me to explain what I was doing? His acceptance of what I had done—it disturbed me more than if he had questioned me. Something was going on here.

"Why don't you step into my office?"

The somber automatrons went back to their desks as I approached the towering Huppington. He shook my hand with strength acquired from years of practice … and gave me that odd look again. What was it all about? It wasn't a suspicious look; it was more like he thought he knew me from somewhere but wasn't quite sure where.

"Have a seat," he said as he stumbled forward into the room. I offered him a hand. When he took it, I glanced down at his shoes. They were the newest brand of Karlton Heated Boots™, which stretched inches above the knee, and were rectangular in shape. So Sylvester had the same boots as the person who walked beneath that cluster of apple trees, I thought to myself. I had to see if it matched the muddy footprint, so I slowly blinked my eyes, snapping a Yabble© photograph. Then, with a rapid blink, I entered it into the Detective Database. It could take up to thirty minutes to process. I had to stall him.

I sat across from Sylvester's mahogany desk as he ambled over to his large, brown leather chair. There was one window in the office, overlooking the line of apple trees, and one colossal painting, which hung behind the desk: President Lapin, wearing white, in the middle of the stock exchange, was standing with confidence, arms at her sides, head tilted, a serious face. She was oblivious to the stockbrokers around her, scurrying from place to place, with wide, open-mouthed smiles. Behind her in fluorescent was the stock ticker, with a green arrow pointing up. Here was a painting that was legally commissioned by The Nation. Every book Sylvester ever published was supported by The Nation. He was a tycoon in an industry that could never produce creative books. Yet according to The Chief, this man was also a creator, leading two completely different lives.

Sylvester collapsed in his chair and gave out a heavy sigh, remarking, "I'm not as young as I used to be."

"How old are you?"

"You want to know my age?"

"If you don't mind."

"Seventy-five."

"Oh, you've got years ahead of you."

He smiled. His small eyes curved upward when he smiled, as if his eyes were forming a smile of their own.

"With medicine these days, sure, I could extend my life span a few decades, but one thing medicine can't cure is a tired mind."

"I couldn't help noticing the large painting of the President behind you."

"Oh yes," he said, with a clearing of the throat. "It's been here as long as I have!"

"Would you mind if I took a closer look?" I asked, getting up from the chair.

"Oh, don't bother!" he replied, an alarmed expression in his eyes. "No need to get up. What other questions do you have?"

"Are all your books available for download?"

"Why, of course."

"You don't have any ... *paper* books?"

"Yes, we do have a few paper books but we never bother to look at them, as they no longer serve any purpose, except during moments of nostalgia."

"Where do you keep them?"

"We have an archive in the back of the building. There's really not much to see."

I gazed out the window, thinking about what Sylvester had said. A room in the back of the building? The archive of paper books had to be where I saw that steel door handle behind the cluster of apple trees. Why did the photograph matching have to take so long? It was so easy to get frustrated with UNICÉ. How quickly one gets accustomed to efficiency! It's no wonder The Nation nearly collapsed when UNICÉ disconnected during the Great Fall. I'll never forget how lost people were, not knowing what to do with themselves, with the exception of the skyjumpers, leaping off rooftops and falling to their deaths. Was it that reality hit us too hard—we couldn't bear to live without UNICÉ? Or was it that the reality of our world had altered so much that disconnecting from UNICÉ was disconnecting from reality? I prayed that night that if there was another Great Fall, it wouldn't last as long. I know that for many of us, it was the longest two minutes of our lives. We were terrified. We …

"Who's *we*?" I asked.

"I'm sorry?"

"You said, '*We* never bother to look at them.' So I'm assuming you have a partner of some kind?"

"Why, yes," he replied, with a smile. "My daughter." He hit a button on his desk. "Iryna! There's someone here who I'd like you to meet."

The door to Sylvester's office opened, and in walked Iryna Huppington. She was in her early thirties. She had long, flowing blond hair, her small breasts poked through her red turtleneck, and her hazel eyes landed on me as she entered the room. Iryna wore moldable shoes with adjustable heels—and was still short. She walked with good posture though and held her head high as she approached me, walking with a sort of natural authority, and then shook my hand with surprising vigor.

"Nice to meet you. I'm Iryna." She glanced at Sylvester while putting her hand in her pocket. "So this is *him*?"

"Yes, this is … the reporter."

My glasses shook ever so slightly. I blinked my eyes rapidly and entered the Detective Database. Lo and behold, the footprint beneath the apple tree matched Sylvester's boots. I just needed one more thing, to know for sure that I was dealing with creators.

"Are you married, Ms. Huppington?"

Iryna put her hand to her mouth. "Is this for the article, Mr. Cunningham?"

"It's just that I noticed you have two rings on your fingers, and your bio says that you're not married."

"Oh," she replied. She lifted her hands to glance at the rings. "They were just gifts."

That was when I knew for certain. When I got a good look at Iryna's right hand. I had my proof that they were creators.

"You wouldn't want to marry me, anyway," she muttered under her breath.

"Why not? I mean, beside the fact that I'm already married."

"There you are. Do you have any other questions about our *business*, Mr. Cunningham?"

I looked down. I could stop there, I thought. Excuse myself and thank them for their time. There was no going back once I told them what I knew. But no. I was not afraid. My eyes veered upward, past Sylvester's mahogany desk and wrinkled forehead, to the painting of President Lapin. I had a duty to fulfill.

"When I came here by skytrain," I replied, "I noticed a single footprint at the back entrance to the tower. This seemed odd to the mind of a reporter, and I shrugged my shoulders and made nothing of it. Until I came here. When I came into your office, Mr. Huppington, I noticed that you were wearing heated boots, rectangular in shape, which matched the footprint I had seen earlier."

Sylvester and Iryna exchanged glances.

I lowered my voice to a whisper and said, "I have creative inclinations but I have been afraid to pursue these interests or find myself in prison. I heard about an underground movement of creators and that Sylvester

Huppington himself was part of such a movement."

"I don't know what you're talking about," Sylvester said flatly.

Iryna examined me as if I were a lover she suspected of being unfaithful. "We're not part of any 'underground movement'. We have always been loyal members of The Nation and there's no reason—"

"I thought I was just imagining things … until I met *you*, Iryna."

"Me?" Iryna asked with a snort.

"You shook my hand with a great deal of strength for a small woman and I thought maybe you did some sort of art with your hands, say, sculpture. When I asked if you were married, I wanted to get a glimpse at your hands, hoping you would glance at them instinctively. It was then that I knew you were a creator because I could tell that you had recently worked with your right hand—it was larger than your left so its muscles were more developed."

Iryna peered at me with contempt. The warm friendliness from when we first met was completely gone and replaced with an incredulous fury. But it was Sylvester's contemplative gaze that I met. His small eyes linked with mine.

"How do we know you're not a *cop?*" Iryna asked.

"I snapped a photo of the footprint. Watch my eyes." I took two, slow blinks. "It's deleted. You can check UNICÉ if you'd like. It never existed. And besides, *you* requested me for this interview," I said. "That's the only reason I came here in the first place. Why *did* you request me, Mr. Huppington?"

Sylvester just sat there and looked at me, seemingly at a loss for words. He began to speak, "I, um …" but then fell into a daze.

Iryna finally answered for him, "He gets into these

old spells sometimes. We requested you because of your fine reputation, Mr. Cunningham."

"My fine reputation," I repeated with a smile. Then in a pleading tone, I continued, "I need to be with people like me. What do I have to do to join the movement?"

As I said those words, a strange question came into my head: who are people like me? Are they detectives, like Kenneth, who could kill a beggar out of a false sense of duty? Are they Upperclassmen, who parade themselves with luxury with no real sense of the suffering of others? Around the end of college, I became a detective and married into the Upper Class, and I had identified myself with these groups ever since. But this was before I saw Kenneth kill that beggar and smelled his blood, and when I thought about that day, shame ripped through me like a self-inflicted disease. I no longer knew where or to whom I belonged, and in that moment, I felt the same way as when the dead beggar's *brother* peered into my soul, judging me as a man of a higher class, as a detective ... I shook off the feeling. Everyone goes through midlife crises and then they come out more assured than ever of their life choices. That was all this was.

Sylvester kept studying me. I stared back at him, without showing a hint of weakness. And then a small, strange smile slowly formed on Sylvester's face.

"Movement or no movement, who *are* you, Mr. Cunnigham?" Iryna asked, tilting her head and walking toward the window. "Where did you get this idea of a movement?"

"I hear you need art or writing or some creative piece from the past to join."

She turned, hitting me with her stare. "Are you an artist, Mr. Cunningham? A writer?" Her eyebrows raised, crinkling her forehead.

I found myself picking at the leather on the arm of the chair.

"I'm a poet."

"Mm hmm. And what does a poet do?"

I swallowed hard.

"Writes poetry, of course."

"We have a genius on our hands! Do you know what we do to *rats*, Mr. Cunningham?" She walked over to Sylvester's desk and pulled open a drawer. She pulled out a gun and pointed it at my chest. "What is the structure of a poem?"

I gripped the arms of the chair with my hands.

"Is this really necessary, Iryna?" Sylvester asked, putting his hand on her arm that held the gun. "Why don't you put that down?"

"Let him answer the question," Iryna said, her eyes fixed on me.

"Oh, Iryna …" Sylvester said, shaking his head. "Go ahead, Mr. Cunningham. I'm sure you know this."

I could feel my face turning red. What was I to say?

"Well?" Iryna asked, raising her eyebrows again, a slight smile forming on her lips.

"A poem doesn't have a structure. It is whatever the writer chooses it to be."

Iryna continued glaring into my eyes, the gun steady in her hand.

"All right, Iryna? Are you satisfied?" Sylvester asked.

"No."

"Well, *I* am," Sylvester said. He said those words in a voice I had not detected before, one that was even and firm, the type of voice that conveyed the unusual quality of a person so self-assured that he does not need to prove himself to anyone else. He ordered, "Now put down that gun."

Slowly, Iryna lowered her arm.

I sighed. But I couldn't help questioning why I had been given this case … and if I could handle it. It was my first case, after all.

"Mr. Cunningham," Sylvester explained. "There is no movement, but if there were, anyone who wanted to enter it would have to *prove* himself—in two ways. First of all, he or she needs someone who is already in the movement to verify his identity. And second, he needs to show us his art so we can see that he is genuine. Do you have anything to show us, Mr. Cunningham?"

"Not on me."

"Hm," Iryna grumbled. "Suspicious, I say," she said, looking at Sylvester. "I say we swear him to secrecy and ask he not return. I don't trust him."

"Come back here again, Walter, with some of your writing. Tomorrow at midnight."

"Thank you, Sylvester. And I assure you, I mean no harm."

"We'll see about that," Iryna quipped. "And if you open that clever mouth of yours and tell anyone what you now know, we will not hesitate to do whatever is necessary to keep our secret. Even if that means making a visit to that wife of yours. I hope you know who you're dealing with."

Chapter Six: The Notebook

I could solve cases, uncover the facts, but I didn't know how to be creative. I only told the Huppingtons that I was a creative writer because Walter Cunningham is a journalist. It just seemed to make the most sense. But I was hoping I could expose Sylvester before having to do anything artistic. No luck there. I was forced to write something creative and it had to be "genuine" or else I'd never be let in and get the proof I needed. And having to imagine something out of thin air and put it into words—I had no idea where to start.

If only when I disguised myself as Walter Cunningham, I inherited a new mind as well as body. Then I could write. But then I would not be able to separate Walter from myself. I had to be two people at once—this was the life I had chosen.

As I walked back from Huppington Books™ through the Slums, I looked down the block and spotted Greenswald Park, home to the largest community of beggars in The City. The park was surrounded by a wall of trees, shielding the Upperclassmen from viewing what went on inside. I patrolled Greenswald in my first years on the force and believe me, you don't want to know what goes on in there. The Slums surrounding the police station are Eden in comparison to Greenswald.

On the side of the street across from the wall of trees
was a group of beggar teenagers, rummaging through
the trash by an abandoned building. They were fighting
over leftover French fries. I found myself studying
them, particularly one girl. She had long fingers, and
curly, untamed hair. But it was her wild, gray eyes I
couldn't stop watching. She stood aside from the
others, watching them as if she were a cat waiting for
the right moment to pounce.

I looked beyond them and saw none other than
Kenneth, coming to interrupt my thoughts. He looked
different out of uniform, purple jeans hung loosely
around his legs, his hair uncombed. But I could tell it
was him because of that mischievous smile.

"Hello, *Walter*."

"Hello, Kenneth. What are you doing in the Slums?"

"Let's just say I had an idea where you were going
today." He reached into his pocket and pulled out a
holographic card, which attached to the palm of his
hand like a magnet. On it was his name and a picture
of his face: that irritating smile.

"I'm a private detective now."

"That's great, Kenneth. You're walking around with
your face on a card."

He muttered, under his breath, in a bitter yet strained
voice, "My wife threatened to leave me because I got
the sack ..." his voice trailed off and his eyes wandered,
as he gets in his most human moments. "I'm trying to
make dough as a private detective, but I don't know if
it will be enough to pay off the bank .... If only I could
borrow a little money from a friend."

"I'm sorry to hear that, I really am. But you can't
change what's already happened. I can't lie for you,
anymore."

"Don't act all self righteous, you arrogant prick!"

Kenneth shouted, his temper rising, "You ratted on me because you wanted my job." He took out his liquidator and aimed it at my face. My body trembled. "I took you under my wing and you stabbed me in the back! Revenge, Victor, that'll change everything."

"Don't shoot me, you're already in enough trouble as it is."

"I taught you everything I know."

"Put the gun down. You won't get away with killing another Upperclassman."

"You're only an Upperclassman because of your rich wife!"

"Leave Anji out of this."

"Hit a sore spot, did I? You fucked up my marriage, why shouldn't I fuck up yours?" Kenneth's temper was wild now, his eyes widened, the hand holding the gun shaking. "Goodbye, Victor. It was nice knowing you."

He went to pull the trigger—this is it, I thought—but then shot at the beggars instead. The bullet screamed past my ears, its sulfuric scent pervading the air as small gusts of steam emitted from the burning water, which had dissolved into the wall of the abandoned building. The beggars squealed and ran away, except for the girl with the gray eyes, who was holding the clump of fries in her hand. She dropped them to the ground and stood there, stunned.

"Give me those fries!" Kenneth commanded. The beggar scrambled to pick them up. As she did, a small notebook dropped out of her pocket. Although I couldn't make out what it said, I could see, as she snatched it off the ground, an open page filled from top to bottom with words. Was she a writer?

Kenneth hadn't even noticed. He was cackling. "Do you see this girl?" he asked me, "She's hilarious! Kinda cute too, for a beggar."

"Leave her alone!" I shouted. My face felt hot.

Kenneth put the gun back into his jacket and there was a strange glint in his eye. "Who do you think I am?" he asked, all of the fury gone from his voice. "I was only kidding." He spoke softly, almost pleadingly. "I would never shoot a kid. I have a daughter, remember?"

"Who I've never met!"

"I don't mix business with family. It's the first rule of any detective. Or did you forget that one?"

The beggar tried to hand him the fries. "You don't need to give that to him," I said to her. The girl and I locked eyes for a moment. She couldn't have been older than eighteen. Then she spun around, her hair bouncing off her back as she walked. When she reached the end of the street, she offered some of her food to the other beggars. I could see the top of the notebook sticking out of her pocket. If I could get those writings from her, then I'd have something to show Sylvester. I had to go after her.

"Ya know," Kenneth said, "you paint me out to be some sort of monster. Meanwhile, you were the one who ratted me out." I tried to ignore him, to follow the girl, but he shot his eyes into mine, as if he was possessed, and I had to stare back at his face. He looked bold, even a bit scared, as he added, bitingly, "Ever since ya killed that beggar kid, you've gone soft."

Something inside me snapped. I grabbed him by the neck and threw him against the building. "Don't you tell anyone about that!" I shouted as he gasped for air.

When he began to choke, I let go of him. He flicked a card with his finger; it flipped through the air, floated toward the ground like a falling leaf, and attached itself to my hand.

"Keep it," he smirked. "So you remember this face."

I peeled it off and let it drop to the pavement. As I walked away, I could hear Kenneth's voice behind me.

"You haven't seen the last of me. Don't forget—I have a friend in the TPF!"

When I got to the end of the street, the girl was gone. She must have entered Greenswald Park but I didn't have a weapon, so there was no way I was going in there.

Somehow, I had to write.

But all I knew was UNICÉ. Finally back in my office, I took out my nanokit. I put my left elbow on my knee as if I were about to do a bicep curl and stuck a needle in my arm. I felt my eyelids lift and the nanotron shooting into my brain. I was in the sky. Karlton Heated Boots™ expanded and contracted, warming a foot; Wang's Kimonos™ floated easily, whispering, "The newest variety to sustain your wife's Qi ... "; a man sighed with relief as Bob Comfort's Moldable Pillow™ created a perfect depression for the shape of his head; a book's pages flapped in the breeze, a deep voice reverberating, "Come to the antique store in the Great Mall, where you can relive your past ..." I closed my eyes, slouched in the soft, maroon chair and let the soft breeze hit my cheeks.

"You have a message," spoke the computer, "from The Chief." I listened to The Chief's gravelly voice, "Lester Lincoln will be your second detective. He's meeting you tomorrow night at Huppington Books. Verify him. When you get into the creator's hideout, find where they keep their weapons. Get that evidence, Victor." Sure, once I was in I could verify Lester, but who was going to verify *me*?

There was only one officer I could trust.

"Send message to Lauren McQuade," I said. "Let's play cubes."

"Lauren McQuade is on UNICÉ."

The light blue tint and foamy clouds of the artificial sky melted into a sharp glasslike downward facing triangle that rapidly cut into the earth in less than a second as the brown, fuzzy walls of the cubes room formed around it. The multicolored cubes, which floated inches above a circular table, rose into the air. They spun around, over, under, and through each other in a medley of color. In a matter of seconds, they rested midair, ready to be played.

Lauren appeared in the seat across from me. Lauren was often ridiculed by fellow policemen for being a woman of the law. She wanted to be a detective but people said she was *too* pretty. One of the bolder cops told her she'd do better catching criminals by showing off her tits than firing a gun. When she told him to go screw himself, he replied simply, "They're big." Lauren acted tough. Her aqua eyes, which could melt a man with a single glance, could burrow into those of the officers, as if challenging them to dare offend her any further. But I'd known Lauren for a long time, and understood that in the inside, Lauren was as vulnerable as a child.

The cubes were blocking our line of sight so I moved my head to the right so I could see her, and she tilted her head to the left. When I then moved my head to the left and she to the right, she started to laugh and pushed the cubes to the sides of the room. Her mouth shook as it emitted a sweet, childlike giggle. I hadn't heard that laugh in a long time.

"Congrats on your promotion, Victor!"

"Thanks. Let's start. I'll be green."

"I'll be white."

The cubes morphed into green and white. I motioned to Lauren to go first and she lifted one of her cubes up three spaces and one space to the right so that it was in front of one of mine.

"I gotta ask you something," I said, pulling one of my cubes two spaces down and two to the left so her cube was blocked on two sides. "As I suspected, my new case has to do with an underground movement of creators. The Chief said that he got a tip from someone inside but he wouldn't tell me who he was."

"Or she."

"Are you saying that … because you were on that top secret case before?"

"I'm not saying anything."

"Well, I need to know who he or she is because I have to be verified in order to get into the movement."

Lauren looked at her cube as if she were trying to decide something. Then she reached her hand to it and hesitantly moved it away from my two green ones that were surrounding it.

"Maybe you could befriend someone in the movement?"

"Right, but I don't know anyone …" I thought about that girl with the notebook and could feel a knot forming in my stomach. I didn't want to return to Greenswald Park. Still, I needed those writings.

"Oh, I also have to … bring him some creative writing," I added with a chuckle.

She glanced at me and then back at her cube. "Everyone has a creative side." I didn't know what she meant by that. "Well?" she asked when I didn't say anything. "What happened with Kenneth?"

"I got tired of lying for him. So I told The Chief what really happened on the bank case."

She looked up at me with sudden interest. "But you always lied for him before. Why tell The Chief now?"

"I may never get an opportunity like this again to

become First Detective." I paused. Then I added under my breath, "And he killed a beggar in front of his brother."

She studied me closely with those large, aqua eyes. "I think it's more than the badge. You were angry with Kenneth for killing that beggar, not because you're jealous or wanted his job, but because he's a *cop*."

I stopped for a moment, my hand, about to move a cube, resting midair.

"You're starting to question your work, Victor."

I laughed. Then I lifted one of my cubes from the bottom right corner so it enveloped Lauren's cube, the green swallowing the white. "It's your turn."

"I've questioned my job before," she said, with a shrug of the shoulders, as if what she were saying was completely normal. "I remember that day we first met at the Academy. You told me then that you wanted to be a cop to make a difference. To help people."

"What I remember are the fake badges we designed on UNICÉ when we pretended to be real detectives. They were gold with the engraving of an eagle. Silver letters lined the bottom, spelling: 'DETECTIVE.' They were so similar to the real thing."

"That was fun. But what I'm saying is … now you're questioning if helping people as a cop is even possible in this world."

"The other officers are right. You *are* crazy."

"They just say that because they like me and I'm not interested in them."

"It's still your turn."

"I lost. Let's just talk." She waved her hand in the air and the cubes fell back into their original places.

"Giving up already!" I exclaimed, watching the cubes zoom past my eyes. "I guess I'll get off UNICÉ."

"And go where?"

"Back home."

"Oh, that's right," Lauren said as if just remembering something important. "A new shoe store opened up in the Great Mall. You should take Anji there."

Was that a genuine suggestion or was she implying something about Anji? Half the time I couldn't understand Lauren ... and she was my closest friend. Women are a puzzle that I'm always trying to solve. I thought Anji was the only woman I understood. But I'd soon find out that I didn't even know my own wife.

"You were at the Great Mall?" I asked. "I thought you never left UNICÉ."

"Ha ha," she said mockingly. "Okay, I admit it, I saw an ad for it in virtual shopping. I couldn't afford anything there ... but Anji would like it. See you later."

With that, she vanished into the air. I came back into my office and glanced at the picture of Anji with her chestnut curls. I wasn't about to tell her about the shoe store. She'd ask how I'd heard of it and I couldn't tell her it was from Lauren. Anji was always a little jealous of her since I joined the Academy.

⚘

The beggars had made Greenswald Park their own. The police were less likely to bother them there. Our job was to protect the people; as long as the beggars stayed away from the Upper Class, we had no reason to provoke them. The more beggars who lived in parks, the less confrontations in the streets, and the easier our jobs would be. During their first year on the force, officers were required to patrol Greenswald Park at night. This was a test of wills for any man. I had nearly pushed my memories of those times out of my conscious mind. But sometimes they leaked out of my subconscious and then I couldn't always distinguish between memory and dreams.

Most of the beggars congregated in vast open areas and blockball fields. I was stationed at Granite Point, a tower overlooking one of the most extensive communities of beggars, The Great Slum, which was filled with hundreds of them living in tents. I did everything I could to stay in my tower and avoid entering The Great Slum. It was ridden with disease, hideousness, and filth. My job was to keep a lookout at night to make sure no one ventured far from his or her home or else be shot. I rarely had to shoot though—they were too busy killing themselves. Fights would break out, there'd be arguing, shouts, silence. On my way out in the morning, the smell of blood would waft into my nose and as the sun came up, and I could view The Great Slum in the low light, I'd often find a weapon: a knife or a stick, haphazardly strewn in the grass. Sometimes I'd see a body tossed in the woods. More often than not it would remain there until it decayed and became part of Greenswald Park itself.

Not all the beggars in parks lived in open areas. They put up their tents under trees, between rocks, along streams, on hills. I remember walking into the park on my way to Granite Point, seeing the beggars' homes. I stopped at a tent halfway enclosed by trees where I heard a shout and went to investigate. As I approached, I caught the smell of a kind of meat I couldn't identify. There were wet clothes hanging on a line. When I poked my head inside the tent, wavegun in hand, there was no person in sight, just a candle-lit room with an ornate carpet in the center of the floor. I remember wondering why they bothered with the rug at all, let alone one with an elaborate design—it seemed oddly out of place. My right hand, holding the wave gun, shook, which it often did during those first years on the force. Coming out of the tent, I heard the crackling of a fire, and I saw a father and his two young children. The girl was around eight years old and the boy four. They sat around the fire, cooking a chipmunk on a long stick. The eight-year-old was wrapping her father's wrist with a leaf. It looked as if he had burnt himself in the fire. Seeing me, the girl dropped the leaf with a gasp and started to walk backward toward the trees. I said to her, "It's okay, I won't hurt you. I just heard a scream. Keep the noise down." The family didn't respond; they just stared. As I left, I remember looking back at the tent, the wet clothes blowing in the breeze, the smell of meat evaporating into the air. Even then, I felt an odd compulsion to that family's way of life—how they slept by candlelight, the way the girl bandaged her father's hand. I respected how they cared for each other, how they managed to live. In the strangest way, I envied them.

I woke up in a sweat. Anji was snoring, strands of hair covering her face. I got out of bed and put on my nanojacket. I went into the kitchen, removing food from the freezer, the fridge, the cabinets. I was going for a drive.

The battery was fully charged and ready. I stepped into the circular car pod. The car wasn't locked and I could have sworn that I had locked it the last time I used it. But I was feeling bold, even a little careless; I was giving in to my impulses. All I knew was that I wasn't a creator; I couldn't write. I had to find that girl with the notebook.

"Sedan MHO 3000," I said. "I'll need something safe. With extra locks." The car transformed around me as it descended to the fifteenth floor. The pod door opened. "Start ignition," I said.

67

"Ignition started," the car replied. "Battery at 100% capacity."

"Drive," I said. "To Greenswald Park."

I raced between skyscrapers. I looked through the glass roof and took in the height of The City, the buildings looking as tall and impressive as ever, the smog high above. Then I stared ahead into the darkness, as the car drove between the electric wires that prevented vehicles from rocketing to the sky or plummeting toward the ground. The airpath was so empty that I had the urge to tell the car to drive through the red lights, to ignore the illuminated stop signs. But the car was built to never break the law; it could never make a human error.

I came to an intersection near the park and told the car to descend. The car dipped to the ground and landed on a street surrounding the park. Beggars rose from their slumbers to peer inside at the rare sight. Some refused to move off the street and the car automatically came to a halt.

That was when the tapping began. It was rhythmic, soft, and relentless. Although it was dark, I could see the fingernails hitting my window and the dirty, toothless faces of the beggars. The children, held by their mothers, motioned to their mouths. I took the food I had placed on the passenger seat and stepped out of the car. I was immediately swarmed.

"Back up!" I shouted, taking out my wave gun and shooting it into the air. "One at a time." At the sound of my gun, the beggars backed away. I held out a can of food and a brave one approached me, snatching it out of my hand. I gave something to each of them. But one man was greedy, and he tried to take it all. I pushed him back with the butt of my wave gun and the beggars murmured. "Only one for each of you!" I commanded, and they listened this time, hesitant hands snatching the food from my fingers. I watched as they came up to me, trying to make out their faces, trying to find that girl. She had looked right at me. I couldn't forget those wild gray eyes.

"That's all I've got," I said as a hand brushed against mine, holding nothing but air. They started to swarm me again, reaching out their arms and extending their fingers, grasping at the air. One tried to grab the gun out of my hand so I beamed him. They murmured loudly at the sound. I opened the driver's door and got into the car, trying to shut the door without crushing arms and legs. The beggars wouldn't move from in front of the car. Then the engine sputtered to a halt, and the car said, "Malfunction."

"Not now!" I shouted. I had never learned how to work a car; it had always fixed itself. Flat tires, scratches, dents, they were all automatically fixed without the driver having to do a thing. It was all terribly convenient. The engine was supposed to work "all the time, everywhere," as the ad said, except it could malfunction, but the chances of that were a thousand to one. This is what happens, I thought, when you rely on technology.

All I could hear was the tapping surrounding the car, and when I dared look out the window, I saw the small fingers of children motioning to their mouths over and over. For a moment, I felt helpless, imagining the beggars' fingernails slowly breaking the glass. And then I heard a scream behind me, a high, pubescent, fear-stricken screech—from *in* the car. I turned my head, and there, crouched behind my seat, was Tommy.

Chapter Seven: The King of the Beggars

Tommy opened the door. I snatched my wave gun and got out of the car. It was so dark that I couldn't see him and then, in an instant, a hand hit the back of my head. I felt my gun being stripped, my thoughts became jumbled, and I was unable to reach for my liquidator, my legs stumbled, my vision rose to the night sky, I told myself to get with it, my son is in danger—

"DAD!" Tommy screamed. "Help me!" My eyes adjusted to the darkness and I could make out two beggars dragging him away. I was being held from behind.

"Let go of him!" I pleaded, but my words were useless.

And then the screams stopped. The tapping ceased. The only sound was footsteps—thump, thump. The beggars dragging Tommy watched in stunned silence as a man with a boxy head, bulbous chest, and enormous arms, approached them. He took them by their throats, and in an instant, they dropped to the ground.

I elbowed one of the beggars who held me, freeing up my hand to strike the other in the face. Tommy ran into my arms. He looked down at the beggar I had hit, who lied unconscious on the ground, saying, "You hit him hard, Dad."

I didn't get a chance to respond. The beastly man

ambled slowly toward us. I held Tommy close as he approached. He looked down at my son, and spoke, in a low voice, "Are okay?"

Tommy nodded his head slightly.

"Thank you," I said.

He looked at me with clear, sky-blue eyes, as if he were examining my intentions, my worth. Then step-by-step he walked to the hood of the car, flicked it open, and stuck two giant hands inside. He worked slowly, like a surgeon performing an operation. Then he closed the lid.

"No power. Try now," he said. Then he turned, and walked on. I wanted to give him food or water. But something told me that here was a man who would not have accepted it. As I watched his large figure disappear into the darkness, I thought to myself that I had just met the king of the beggars.

When we got back into the car, Tommy sat in the passenger seat. "Spiraling Tower. Apartment 868," I said, and the front of the car rose toward the sky. I wanted to give it directions, to prove I knew how to get back, but I had to swallow my pride and get my son home safe.

Tommy sat in silence, his eyes glazed and his body shaking. I put my arm around him and told him everything was all right. Like all Upper Class children, Tommy was sheltered. He had seen the Slums from the skytrain but had never been there. But now, he had just come face-to-face with an entirely new reality.

I asked, "Tommy, what were you doing here?"

"I couldn't sleep."

"Tell me the truth." Tommy instinctively looked down and I saw something hidden underneath his shirt. I pulled it out.

I couldn't believe what I held in my hands. A notepad

with a wooden cover, and pages filled with drawings. My son was ... and hiding it from me, from his mother ...

I flipped through it. There was a drawing of Amber, the girl from his class, her hair a deep purple, in pigtails, a small red bruise on her right cheek, and Tommy had accentuated her dimples.

"They're portraits for class," Tommy said, looking at his notepad as if trying to will it back to him with an imaginary force.

"Don't lie to your father." I turned to another drawing, and another, and another.

"You can never *ever* do this again," I said, closing the pad. "You can go to *prison* for drawing. Not only that, but your father is a police officer and your mother is a lawyer. You could get your parents in a lot of trouble. And wood? There are few trees left, you know. So stop hiding things from us, and stop going into my car. I have a very important case to solve and if I do, I could become the head detective—" I stopped. "I'm sorry about what happened, Tommy."

"What were you doing with those beggars?" He had seen me. He had seen me giving food to the beggars.

"I just felt the need to—" I stopped. I tried giving to the beggars and look at what happened. This wasn't the answer. This wasn't what I had to do to fill the void in my life. It wasn't worth it for the safety of my family. Besides, helping the beggars would do nothing for solving the case, unless it gave me an in with Sylvester and the creators. I had to set my priorities straight, get my head right. I had to get that badge.

"Why do they have to live like that? When we have everything we want ..." Tommy trailed off.

"I know. But this is how the world works. Your mother has shielded you for too long. And so have I. Maybe, in a weird way, what happened tonight was good for you. You may not understand that now, I know. But you will." I put the pad between my seat and the door.

"Who else have you shown this to?"

"Amber."

"Tommy, you shouldn't show these to *anyone*."

"But I like her!" he exclaimed with sudden emotion. He looked down despondently. "When I told her I liked her, she said her *dad* won't let her go out with boys. She even said she likes me and that my drawing was 'sweet.' Pff. What does it matter, anyway?"

So that's what Tommy wanted. A girl, just like any other boy his age.

"That's why you drew? To show Amber?"

"Because it felt … I dunno. I liked doing them." He paused. "Can I have it back then," he said quickly, before I could interrupt, "eventually? So I can show Amber?"

"Absolutely not! Have you heard a word I've said?" Tommy had never talked to me about girls before. So I said softly, "You know, Tommy, I wasn't the only guy who liked Mom. I had to win her."

"What did you do?"

"Your mom was so beautiful, I was almost speechless around her. She was always with this other guy who was bigger than me—she knew him from high school. But I loved her. So I told myself to be brave and I asked her out. Everyone gets rejected, Tommy. It's telling a girl that you like her that's the hard part. I couldn't do it until I met Mom."

"Really? Weren't you in college by then?"

"Yeah," I said. "I was shy."

We sped down the street, watching skyscrapers as they passed through the glass roof of the car. I tried to swallow down the pain of old memories. I was just trying to make Tommy feel better. I had had plenty of girlfriends.

"Dad? What I still don't understand is why the beggars have to live like that."

"All right. We've shielded you long enough and so have your teachers. It's about time you knew some realities. There's President Lapin, right? She's at the top. She keeps us secure but will do anything to hold onto power. Directly working for her is the Technological Police Force. You never *ever* want to get in the way of the TPF."

"Why not?"

"Because they'll do whatever the President says and you don't want to get in the way of power. If you ever hear … " I took a deep breath, trying to push away the past, " … a helicopter, either run or hide. Then there are the corporations: insurance companies, the National Bank, and Yabble©, which has monopolized the Internet. 51% of what the corporations earn goes to the government. But in essence, the corporations and the government—they are one in the same. They control everything."

I paused as my mind wandered to Huppington Books™. Why would Sylvester want to put his position of power in jeopardy to hide creators—*illegals?* What was it that attracted him to art so much that he was willing to make this sacrifice? I found my eyes drifting down to Tommy's pad and I felt a compulsion to look at it again.

"And then there's us?"

"That's right. Then there's the Upperclassmen: business magnates, bankers, Stocks Street executives, real estate owners, insurers, lawyers, Hollywood producers."

"What are detectives?"

"Well, I guess you can say we're part of the middle class, but really, besides us and the firemen, there isn't much of a middle class. There is a lower class though. We never see the lower class because they live among themselves. They own small shops and restaurants, even their own apartments—a self-sustaining community. But they don't bother Upperclassmen, so they're of no concern to the police. On the bottom are the beggars. Sometimes they get food from lowerclassmen."

"So that's why you were giving to the beggars? Because they're on the bottom?"

"Yeah, I guess that's why. But look what happened. I put you in danger. This system we have in place keeps everything in order. Everyone plays his or her role in society. It's always been this way. There have always been the rich and the poor. It's always been hard for the poor to move up in class; it's ingrained in their communities and schools. What made things worse for the beggars was the introduction of the automatrons. The robots took all the menial jobs and there was no use for beggars anymore from a societal standpoint. It's sad, I know, but we have to accept our lot in this world. The beggars are not only desperate but they're envious of the Upperclassmen. That's what makes them dangerous." I looked up through the roof of the car. The white blinking light was there, as always, flashing through the sky.

"You see The Guardian? As you know, it's there to make sure other nations don't try to attack us. It's there for self-defense."

Self-defense. I had to learn it on my own at the age of fourteen the day Marty Milfinjer stole my lunch and I socked him squarely in the jaw. I never had a father figure who taught me how to behave. How was I supposed to know how to raise a son?

"You saw what I did to that beggar?"

"Yeah. You hit him hard, Dad. Like in a virtual game."

"Form your hand into a fist." Tommy gave me a skeptical look but he did it. "You have to tighten it as hard as you can before you hit someone. This way you won't hurt your hand." Tommy held out his fist. I put my hand around it. "Harder." His hand shook under mine. "Good. Then put your weight behind the punch. Lean into it. And remember, I'm only telling you to do this in *self-defense*. Don't hit anyone otherwise. Do you understand?"

"Yes, Dad."

I looked up at the Spiraling Tower, swirling into the sky. "All right, we're almost home. Don't tell Mom about what you saw tonight, okay?"

He paused for a moment. "Okay. Then can you not tell Mom about the drawings?" My eyes drifted again toward the pad.

"Fine. Hey, guess what? It's past midnight. You're officially thirteen years old." And not only that—I had to be at Huppington Books™ by midnight the next day and I still didn't have a piece of creative writing.

"How did you *do* them?" I asked.

"What do you mean?"

"I mean, what makes you want to … draw?"

"I promise, Dad, I won't do it anymore."

"You better not. But what I mean is, what is it that makes you want to do something … creative?"

"I just do it to get stuff off my mind," he said effortlessly, shrugging his shoulders. "If I like something. Or if something's bothering me. And I try to make it nice."

"Where did you get the pad?"

"Take a guess, Dad. The only place in The City where you can get whatever you want."

Chapter Eight: The Mountain

The Mountain was a world unto itself. No other building in The City compared with its height, a 6500-foot peak that reached to the heavens, or its impenetrability, indestructibly built with carbon tubing. With the ozone layer depleting, the sun would cut through the smog and reflect off The Mountain, changing its silver exterior to a sharp bright yellow in the heat of the day, and to deep oranges and reds during sunrises and sunsets. It was energized by solar panels. Ailerons ran the full length of the tower to redirect the winds so as to lessen structural vibrations. Seventy thousand people lived in The Mountain, some of whom hadn't left for years. There were even those who grew up there, were schooled there, grew old there.

The residents, including the "lifers," lived at the so-called "peak" of The Mountain, the 500th to 800th floors. As I rode there on the skytrain, I gazed at those upper floors, wondering if the lifers even knew about the Slums below. At the apex was the Sky Theater, illuminating movies onto the sky. Tommy once asked me if that was why actors were called "stars."

The skytrain sped along its track to a portal on the 100th floor of The Mountain. There were only ten portals in the entire building. It was designed that way so visitors would have to ride through the Entertainment

District and Vacation Land if they wanted to go to the Great Mall, and so that the residents would be less tempted to leave.

When I arrived, the skytrain's glass doors opened, I passed through the head scanner, and I stepped onto the crowded mechanized walkway toward the septuple-decker elevators. Tommy had bought his pad at the antique shop in the Great Mall, so that's where I was headed. I avoided taking the automatron driven computer pods that sped people around each floor; they were so crowded that it was difficult to breathe without getting a taste of the musky odor of the person in front of you. Standing beside me on the mechanized walkway were three girls babbling about how much they loved a movie starring Kelly Karr. A group of bird-watchers with hats and nanoculars were looking over maps of the Wild Forest. A few actors from the government-sponsored theater were practicing their lines for a play promoting the magnificence of UNICÉ. I thought of Anji and how she always wanted to perform on the stage of The Mountain Theater.

As I approached the elevators, I looked at the three-dimensional floor chart, which listed the Great Mall under floors 200–399. There was another chart with countless listings under each heading, and it took a good minute until I could find the words that read: "Antique Store: 234." I stepped off the walkway and into one of the elevators, shoving my way to the voice panel to say the number of my floor. The elevator sped upward and stopped at the 145th floor, "Ski Hill," where a group of teenagers entered, dressed in winter jackets, ski boots, and holding skis. They were talking about what trails they planned to ski the next day. At the 171st floor, "The Beach," a family came in, water dripping from their bathing suits, which covered their bodies from shoulder to ankle. The mother asked the father if she looked tan while their daughter tugged on her mother's sleeve, shaking with excitement, for she had seen a whale.

"I want to see dolphins next time, Mommy!" the girl shouted with glee. "Are they as big as whales?"

"Just look it up on UNICÉ, sweetie," her mother replied.

At the 234th floor, I sidled between the girl and a pair of snowy skis to get back on the mechanized walkway that led into the Great Mall. I passed by clothing store after clothing store, watching throngs of women walk in and out. The antique shop was one of the smallest stores on the floor and there wasn't a single person inside. I stepped off the walkway and came to the front of the store, peering into its glass window at the objects put up for display.

There were notepads of all different shapes and sizes, different color pens, and an old typewriter. I had never seen one before. It had round keys that looked like buttons on strings. It was hard to believe that people had to memorize a random pattern of letters and used their fingers to form words. The machine wasn't even attached to a computer; instead, it had a spot where a sheet of paper could be printed, and there was a small lever on its side. Beside it was a pile of notebooks and I spotted Tommy's pad with its wooden cover. I suddenly realized that I had been gazing into the display for some time, and I quickly looked around to see if anyone had seen me, then went inside.

The store smelled like an aging forest and was crammed with ancient objects: cameras as long as my arm, iPods. I glanced at the time on a digital watch: 3:00 PM—nine hours until I had to bring a piece of creative writing to Huppington Books™. I marched toward a counter in the back where an old man was sitting on a wooden stool, which looked like it would break any minute, its four legs rocking back and forth as the old man shifted his weight. Although the man did not look content, hunched forward with a grimace on his face, he seemed complacent on that stool, like a resident of an old home that was falling apart, but still held indefinable sentimental value.

"Coming to sell?" he asked.

"Sell?"

The man looked annoyed. "Yes. Do you have something you would like to sell?"

"I'd like to buy a pad. From the display, with the wooden cover. And pens."

The man grunted, slowly getting off his stool. He trudged to the front as if every step he took was strenuous and difficult. He took the pad from the display, as well as blue, red, green, silver, and black pens, and handed them to me without meeting my eye. I waited a moment for him to return to the counter, but he just stood there and put out his hand.

I paid the old man and left the store. As I came to the mechanized walkway, I took a quick backward glance at the typewriter. For a brief moment, I caught myself wondering what it felt like to press down on those keys.

❧

When I came back to the apartment, I smelt the devil's food cake Anji was baking for Tommy's birthday. It was the same scent that welcomed me the day I met Kenneth's wife.

Soon after I was assigned to Second Detective, with the badge in sight for the first time, Kenneth invited me over his home for dinner. It was a windy day; the breeze was so strong that I could feel the skytrain sway ever so slightly. The devil's food cake was baking as I entered the apartment, its walls painted a bright yellow. Dora greeted me with a kiss on the cheek and I got a whiff of her minty breath. As I sat down for dinner, she smiled at me, a smile that was a bit too wide, one of those smiles when someone stretches the sides of her mouth to make a good impression. I could tell by that smile that something wasn't quite right with Dora; the walls of her apartment were a bit *too* bright, her breath slightly *too* minty. Yet on the surface, everything seemed normal. Kenneth and I discovered that we both played cubes. Dora described the ingredients that she stuffed inside the turkey (rosemary, garlic, and thyme). She loved traditional cooking, but wanted a change. With a wink to Kenneth, Dora told me she wanted a child, and Kenneth rolled his eyes playfully, and then held his wife's hand.

It was when Dora served the devil's food cake that I first noticed another side to Kenneth. He bought a gift for her—a virtual cooker, which worked faster than a zapster and could boil, broil, bake, stew, roast, fry, grill, sauté, defrost, freeze, reheat, braise, and fricassee, triggered by the sound of a hushed voice from up to thirty feet away—and this upset her. "With all our financial problems, you shouldn't have bought it!" she exclaimed suddenly at the dining room table. I could see the expectant expression on Kenneth's face dissolving into confusion and then rage. The cake was burnt, he claimed, and he picked up the plate and threw it against the wall, the chocolate smearing against the yellow wallpaper like a squashed bumblebee. I realized then that Kenneth had a wild temper. I excused myself to the bathroom as Dora wiped the cake off the wall. In the cabinet above the toilet, I saw, unmistakably, a bottle of anti-depressants.

Only later would I learn that Dora became hooked on those pills. The rumor among the officers was that she was considered unfit to raise their daughter and was put in an institution. Kenneth began putting all his energy into his work, as if somehow that would gain back his wife's happiness. When his wife returned from the hospital months later, she found that she had been replaced at work, and they fell into serious financial trouble.

Over the next few years, Kenneth's temper grew worse and he became distant from the other detectives, including me. I'll never forget what happened when one officer cracked a joke about his daughter. Kenneth, his eyes captured in a sort of possessed, uncontrollable, and desperate rage, hit the officer with the butt of his gun and nearly killed him. No one talked about Kenneth's family ever since. And I haven't met his daughter. Don't know if I ever will. He's never even mentioned her name.

Anji shut off the oven and we came into Tommy's room with his birthday present. He ripped off the glowing wrapping paper and then opened the box, which was shaped like a liquidator. Inside was a videogame the size of a pin, which fit perfectly inside a nanotron. I loved to watch my son's eyes the moment he opened up his presents. But this time, when Tommy saw the miniscule videotron, "Richard Pellman: Virtual Fight 12," he looked sullen, disappointed. I couldn't understand why.

Anji noticed too. She said to me, out of the side of her mouth, "I thought you said that was what he wanted."

I replied, out of the side of my mouth, "He said it was."

"You're right in front of me!" Tommy exclaimed.

"This *is* what I wanted. Thanks, Mom and Dad."

"Of course, sweetie," Anji said. Tommy cringed at the sound of "sweetie"—the same word Amber used when she rejected him. "Come eat your cake!" Anji exclaimed, leaving to the kitchen.

"What's the matter?" I asked Tommy. "You said in class that you wanted this."

"I did. But after seeing those beggars, it feels funny."

Chapter Nine: Tapping into the Creative Mind

I couldn't shake off that feeling of something missing. The feeling that compelled me to the typewriter, as if somehow through writing I could fill that void. What a ridiculous notion! It was almost comical and I had to dismiss any thought of it immediately. I couldn't veer too far into the creative mind—that was the fear that prevented me from buying that pad until now, that stopped my hand from putting the pen to the page. I had to come up with something that seemed genuine, so I could get into the art movement and obtain the evidence that The Chief desired.

I opened the pad's wooden cover and stared at the first page. I had only five and a half hours until I had to be at Huppington Books™, and I didn't know how to begin. So I went onto UNICÉ. I needed help and I had only one friend who I could trust.

"Lauren, transmit to my office. It's important. I need your help."

"Me? Come to your house? As an image?"

"To my office, yes."

There was a moment of silence.

"Okay."

As I was putting the nanokit away, Lauren transmitted to my office. She was wearing a tank top and shorts. Lauren rarely dressed in fancy clothes. The only jewelry she ever wore was a pair of small, silver hooped earrings that her grandmother, and then her mother, had passed down to her. She hardly ever wore makeup. She looked like a different woman on the day we graduated from the force, when she displayed a hint of sky-blue eye shadow, which made her aqua eyes look bluer, and wore red lipstick that made her lips remarkably enticing. But Lauren didn't need makeup. She always looked pretty.

"Is there any place I can sit?" she asked, looking around.

"Here," I said, getting up. I turned the chair so it faced her and I was standing behind it. She walked toward it and sat, her upper back leaning into my fingers. It felt sort of nice, my hands sinking into her hologram. She turned her head and shot me a quick smile.

"I still need someone to verify me," I said.

She stopped smiling and looked forward, saying, "I know who tipped off The Chief. And that officer can never go back there. I'm sorry."

I walked around the chair and stood in front of her. "I'm way over my head with this case. And I have no one else to talk to."

She gave me a look. "What about your wife?"

I looked over at Anji's picture. "If I tell her anything, I'd be putting her in danger."

"But with *me* it's fine."

"You're a cop, Lauren, you live a life of danger. Besides, you know me well. You were right—I was questioning things about being a detective. And now I need your help." She swung her foot in the air so that it brushed against my leg as she tried to hide a smile. "I have to bring a poem there tonight. The thing is, I don't know how to write it. A policeman's job is to react and then take action. I don't know how to do anything else."

"All right then," she said, "We'll tap into your creative mind."

"Well, it just needs to *seem* genuine—"

"There is a technique I know from ... a poet I once arrested. You're going to go onto UNICÉ and listen to the news. Close your eyes. Then when you hear a word that strikes you, say it. I'll be recording."

"Okay ... but how does that make a po—"

"Do you trust me?"

"Yes."

"Then do it."

Her image vanished into the air.

I stuck a needle into a fresh vein in my upper arm and was back again, in the clouds, on the soft maroon chair.

"Lauren, you there?"

"I'm here, Victor."

"News."

The bald head of the newsman appeared in front of me. I closed my eyes.

"Headline story. The case of *the Environmental Defense Group vs. Huppington Books*™ went to trial today at The City Courthouse." The words were going so fast. I'm supposed to repeat just any word I hear? I didn't get this. Plus I couldn't stop listening to the actual story. "The trial will decide the fate of our national forests and the paper book industry. This is the second time the EDG has sued a client of Grumm LLP. The first time was in fact the only loss that the firm ever had. Even worse, Mr. Grumm was accused of tampering with evidence, scarring his reputation for the rest of his career." They always have to bring this up. Why is Dallas Grumm always such big news?

"Victor, what's going on?"

"He's speaking too fast."

"Just don't think about it, Victor, and *react*. Turn off your mind."

I shut my eyes again.

"Today, the EDG argued that there's something wrong in a world where your …" I felt my mouth moving, but I couldn't hear what I was saying, "'*something wrong in a world where your*' trees are in danger '*in danger*' of being destroyed for '*for*' an industry that is collapsing and often associated with illegal activities, such as engaging in creativity '*creativity*.' Huppington Books™ insists that they don't dare let out '*don't dare let out*' books not commissioned by The Nation and that the EDG can keep '*keep*' trees inside '*inside*' an environmental shield. It is this '*this*' reporter's feeling '*feeling*' that the judge will decide in favor of the EDG since the fall '*the fall*' of the paper book industry is inevitable '*is inevitable*.'"

"Come back, Victor."

My vision was blurry when I opened my eyes. I could see the reporter fading into a cloud.

"Wow, Victor. I had no idea you had thoughts like these."

"What thoughts? I just rambled off words."

"That was your subconscious talking. How did it feel?"

"Like I was in a trance. Is it any good?"

"No. It's absolute dribble. Now I'm gonna repeat what you said, with a bit of editing on my part. Store it and then when you get back to your office, write it in that pad of yours. Yes. I saw it on your desk. Ready?"

"How did you know about this, Lauren? You can tell me the truth."

"Just listen—"

Something's wrong
in a world
where you're in danger
for creativity.

Don't
dare
let out.
Keep inside
this feeling.

The fall is inevitable.

I put the pen down. Looked at the words I just wrote. They were so simple and so few—how could *this* get me into Sylvester's movement? And what was that about my subconscious talking? That was such bullshit. What was amazing is how my ramblings actually made some sort of sense; Lauren must have manipulated them in some way. These words couldn't have come from a detective's heart.

But it seemed genuine. And something a creator would write. And that was all that mattered.

The door to my office opened. I jumped out of my seat, darted toward the closet to grab my liquidator. Iryna's voice, "I hope you know what you're dealing with," echoed in my head. As I was reaching my arm into the closet, I caught a glimpse of the intruder and stopped. It was Anji.

"Who was in here?" My wife's eyes were digging into mine. The chestnut strands that outlined her face looked less like the luring curls that compelled me to meet her lips and more like curved daggers aimed at my heart.

"Oh, hi. You don't usually come in here so I thought …"

"Who was in here?"

"Lauren. It was for work."

"Mm hmm. How interesting. I just got a message from Kenneth. He told me you've been seeing quite a lot of her recently." Her voice was forceful, but I could hear the hurt hidden beneath it.

"Well, she's involved in the case, Anji. And don't listen to—"

"How can I trust you, Victor? You hide everything from me." She gave me such a piercing stare, the one she uses in court, that I was at a loss for words. "Always spending time with her. And now she comes to our *home!* That's not work, Victor! Why was she *here?*"

"Don't listen to Kenneth!" I shouted, a bit desperately.

"Don't evade my question!" Her gaze was fierce, her voice unwavering. Then when I didn't respond, she shouted, "Go to hell!"

"Listen to me," I said, without raising my voice, but rather, speaking firmly in a deliberate tone, choosing my words carefully. It takes me a minute to gather my thoughts and collect evidence—but once I do, there's no one more convincing than me. "I've taken Kenneth's job as First Detective. He feels like I've betrayed him. That's why he said that to you." I met her stare, and continued, "Lauren *had* to come here for work. I would *never* be involved with another woman. And to tell you the truth, I'm pissed that you'd think I would do that. You should know me well enough by now."

Her caramel irises examined me intently but my gaze was fiercer, stronger, angrier. "Kenneth *said*—" she started to say, but then hesitated, "that you've been seeing her …" Her voice dropped, tears swelled up in her eyes, and she couldn't finish her sentence. Then in a cracked voice, looking at the floor, she muttered, "I'm sorry."

"Come here."

She rushed toward me and put her arms around me, her soft face against my chest. I lifted her head and kissed her gently. Then she put her lips to mine, flinging the hair out of her face. Her mouth was wet, her cheek moist against the palm of my hand. It was the most passionate embrace we had had in a long time.

I looked into her eyes, which were teary and brown, like melting caramels. "I will be out late tonight. And it'll be this way until the case is solved. But you and Tommy come first, Anji, you know that. I will be there to protect you, no matter what. I promise." I said it with as much strength and force as I had before, but I thought about the danger that my family was in, with Kenneth and the creators, and for an instant, I couldn't help but second-guess everything I just said.

"I'll remember that promise, Victor." She held me close. "Be careful. I wish you would tell me where you're going. It's hard for me, you know."

"I can't do that. But you know what? I don't have to be there until midnight so ... let's have a night out together. Let's see a show."

Chapter Ten: A Play and a Poem

The Mountain Theater was extravagant in every sense of the word. The walls, seats, and curtains that covered the stage, keeping the set a secret, were all a sharp, blood red. A chandelier hung in the center of the grandiose hall, with lights that simmered, and arms that curved and flowed like those of an octopus. In the center above the stage, for all to see, was the face of President Lapin, the large, somber, charcoal-colored eyes, the thin, static lips.

The play was about a simple farmer, and it took place in the recent past. All Joe knew was the lay of the land. He carried a pocketknife with him the whole play, insisting he could use it to survive in the wild. "There is no need to embrace technology if one has a knife," he pathetically repeated, until the day he chugged a bottle of whiskey and stabbed his own daughter. "From then on," he proclaimed with force, "I realized the error of my ways!" He discovered the wonders of UNICÉ and joined the "real world." In his closing monologue, he stated, "I used to believe that technology was our ruin. That if we rely too much on it, we will lose remnants of the past. But now I see the truth. Man invented a spear and he relied on that spear to survive. Nothing has changed. Just as we relied on that spear, or on automobiles, or on smartphones, we rely on UNICÉ. It is part of the human condition. All I can do is not be an outlier; I must join society. And I thank President Lapin for instilling a sense of pride in the people of our great Nation." The curtain closed, and a voice, monotone but clear, announced, "This was the last man to join UNICÉ and from then on, the country was unified under our great leader."

The crowd erupted in applause. I could see in the wistful smile on Anji's face as she clapped her hands that she felt a special thrill while watching others perform; she lived vicariously through them. Yet she also envied actors—wanted to be them. Behind that expression of joy in her face was an intense feeling of regret. She had given up her dream for her father, her work, her family. I believed that she had put her dreams aside for good.

It was a fine performance by the actor who played Joe the Farmer. It was a fine show, with beautiful costumes, and elaborate sets. But there was a voice nagging me, deep inside, that everything was *too* fine. That something wasn't right. That we were being fed information like animals fattened at a slaughterhouse. That there was some impending doom for all of us. But as I always did, I pushed back that voice, that feeling, and applauded along with the crowd. "Don't dare let out/keep inside this feeling." These were the words I had written in my poem, and I would stick by them. For there were more important things in this world, I told myself. Anji was happy. And so was I.

I held my wife's hand (I couldn't remember the last time I had done so in public) as we made our way into the hallway that led toward the coatroom and the septuple-decker elevators. We passed by two men in a heated conversation. One wore an oversized shirt that nearly hung to his knees and had a scraggly beard;

the other was dressed in a translucent blue tie and a perfectly groomed suit.

"If you remove something that is manmade," the bearded man was saying, "and we cannot survive, then humankind has reached a very dangerous state, indeed. A tipping point, if you will. Do you not agree?"

People gasped around them and Anji tightened her grip on my hand. But I stopped walking and listened. "Let's go," Anji whispered in my ear. But I thought about my family having dinner, lost on UNICÉ, detached from the world, and I remembered The Great Fall, the skyjumpers who tossed themselves off rooftops across The City, unable to live when UNICÉ stopped functioning for just two minutes, and I found my mind wandering, and I thought the impossible: what would happen if UNICÉ failed for good?

"Come *on*," Anji insisted.

I let go of her hand. "Go to the coatroom," I said, distracted, "I'll meet you there."

She grunted and walked on.

"What you are saying is blasphemous!" the man in the suit exclaimed. "I suggest you stop *this instant!*"

"Why should I? You wrote this play. Shouldn't you be questioned for what you have done?"

"For what I have *done?*" The writer's eyes lit up in a fury. I noticed an orange tint in his eye, something that only develops from overuse of UNICÉ.

And then I heard a scream. It was Anji. She was standing in front of the coatroom with a liquidator pointed at her head.

Holding the gun was Kenneth. In his eyes was that look of uncontrollable, reckless rage that I had seen so many times before. But this time, something was different. His hair looked stringier than usual, his clothes dirtier. His expression more desperate.

I approached cautiously. Kenneth had his arm around my wife's shoulder, holding her like a prized possession. Some of the remaining people in the hall stood against the blood-red walls, watching us with horror; the others snuck out quickly as I spoke. "You're in a public place, Kenneth." I tried reasoning with him. There was still a shred of reason in that head of his, wasn't there? "You'll never get away with this. Put down the gun and tell me what happened."

"My wife left me!"

"Oh *no*."

"That's right—she kicked me out of my own home! I lost everything. And all because you stabbed me in the back. Just so you could get a promotion, you selfish prick! And now, as you did to me, I'm going to take your wife away from you."

Just then, a laser shot past my ear and into Kenneth's shoulder. He fell to the ground.

The man with the scraggly beard stuck a laser pistol on his belt, hidden beneath his oversized shirt, and wrapped two electronic handcuffs around the wrists of the stunned Kenneth. Only TPF officers have handcuffs like that. Before pulling Kenneth out of the theater, he turned to the writer of the play, and commented, "You are a faithful member of The Nation. Fine work."

Anji was in my arms, breathing erratically. Her salbutamol jacket had fallen out of her purse and to the floor. I wrapped it around her and held her until her asthma subsided. And then she looked into my eyes.

"After all you said, Victor, you didn't protect me. You left me alone. Already, you broke your promise."

"I—I was ..." My unfaltering confidence, the forcefulness of my voice, it was gone.

Anji's bewildered brown eyes changed into impenetrable stones. She slipped her arms off my shoulders. She walked ahead of me, something she does when she's angry, and I followed her, out of the theater, along the mechanized walkway, through the silence of The Mountain's septuple-decker elevator ride, into the tenseness of the skytrain, and all the way into the satin sheets of our bed. It was only then that I spoke, to the curve of her back. Two words I hate to say.

I'm sorry.

Her only reply was silence.

I went to my office and reported the incident to The Chief, who told me the TPF had Kenneth in their custody. As you know, when someone is taken by the TPF, he almost always disappears. From what I've heard from officers with friends in the TPF, most of the people who they don't shoot on the spot are put behind bars in a penitentiary far from The City. That was where I thought Kenneth was taken, and I believed I would never see him again.

I received a message from Lester Lincoln, my recently assigned Second Detective, "Hey Victor, I'm coming to Huppington Books™ under the name of 'Marcus Van Dermeen.' I'm a banker. Verify me. You should've seen the look on Huppington's face when I showed him the photographs I took. They're a bunch of pictures of pigeons and he totally bought it. This art stuff is such bullshit. See you in half an hour."

It was only thirty minutes until midnight—and still I had no one to verify me. I would have to convince them I was a creator. I wasn't bringing a weapon— I'd activate my bulletproof vest and wound treaters if necessary; instead, I took the pad. I was going to Huppington Books™ armed with a poem.

❧

Iryna's hazel eyes did not leave my face as I read my writing. She stood next to Sylvester, who was at his desk, listening intently. It was weird to read the words out loud—I felt self-conscious, even vulnerable, and then when I finished, I was relieved. They had no reaction at first. Sylvester's expression was blank. It was as if they were mulling over my words, tasting them with their tongues, judging if the flavor was to their liking. I looked at the painting of the President at the stock exchange. I felt like praying to it, 'I'm doing my duty to The Nation, please help me in return.' With no weapons, I felt exposed. I stood there, listening for a response, feeling like Adam after he ate from the tree of knowledge, awaiting the wrath of God.

Finally, Sylvester smiled. "Very nice, Walter."

"But you know," Iryna interjected, "that you need someone in the group to verify your identity. We need to know that you are who you say you are. So I'm sorry, but unless there's someone—"

Iryna was interrupted by a low, masculine voice: "Know him."

There, standing in the doorway of Sylvester's office, was the man who had saved Tommy. His large stature consumed the space of the doorway, his earthy smell lingering into the room. His voice sounded different from before though I couldn't pinpoint what it was. Did I detect a foreign accent? His sky blue eyes met mine, speaking a moment of warning. Why was this man sticking his neck out for me a second time?

Iryna's face had turned a cherry red and her eyes were wide with shock as she turned to face the man, and asked, "What are you doing, Vivek?"

"Saw him. Helping beggars."

Yes, it was an accent, from Eastern Europe, like I had heard in movies. He must have been masking his voice to protect his identity.

"Are you sure it was *him*?" Iryna asked.

"Yes. This man. Reporter."

He had seen *me*, not Walter Cunningham. I studied him suspiciously, but he would not meet my eyes again. Iryna, redder than ever, marched out from behind Sylvester's desk to the doorway. As she brushed by Vivek, he tried to take her hand but she pushed it away and left the room.

"Emotional girl," Vivek said. "Need Vivek to lift painting now?"

Sylvester sat up in his chair. "Now, Walter. You do know that there is no going back at this point. By joining us, you are putting yourself ... your family in danger."

I knew it more than Sylvester realized. If the creators found out who I really was, they'd probably kill me. And if The Chief ever thought I had become manipulated into becoming one of them—then the *cops* would be against me, and the TPF. And in the middle of it all was my wife and son and they couldn't ever know.

Sylvester's automatron opened the door and in walked Lester Lincoln. Lester had a gaunt face and lengthy body. I remember how at the Academy, he tried to cheat off me on the police exam and pleaded when I refused to help him, nearly getting us both in trouble. Lester was never the brightest of the bunch, and the only reason he became Assistant Detective was because of his bold, unyielding reputation among high officers whose feats he made sure to praise.

"Do you know this man?" Sylvester asked me. "He told me you would verify him." I looked at the wiry, emaciated individual, looking down at me as if I held his life in his hands. And I did.

Lester came up to me. "Walter Cunningham, good to see you." I could feel Sylvester watching. I was pissed at The Chief. He had sacrificed my mission by bringing this fool onto the case.

Lester put out his hand. I gave his bony fingers a tight squeeze.

"Marcus Van Dermeen, yes. He's my banker."

"All right then," Sylvester said. "You have both shown me genuine art and have been verified."

"Go inside?" Vivek asked. "I want to play." Play? What was he talking about?

"Yes, it's time," Sylvester said, looking at Lester and then at me. "Welcome to the Art Resistance Movement. Iryna! We're going in."

Iryna came into the office a different woman. Her long, flowing, beautiful blond hair was gone, and replaced with short, brown clumps that stopped just below her ears. Her hair was barely visible, though, beneath the black-and-white striped bandanna she wore around her head. She was dressed in tattered jeans and an oversized button-down flannel long-sleeve shirt. Her moldable shoes were replaced by small round brown loafers with a buckle strap. Without the moldable shoes with their adjustable heels, she was barely five feet, but she still looked tall. She gazed upward at the powerful Vivek and handed him a large black case. He put his arm around her and she leaned her head onto his chest and for a moment, she closed her eyes.

Sylvester pointed at the painting behind him. "Vivek, it's time to lift now."

"Oh, I'll help—" Lester began.

Sylvester turned to face him. We were so close to

getting in. He better not have blown it. "No. I'd rather Vivek do it." I glared at Lester. "Would you mind, Vivek?"

"Yes, of course, Sylvester," Vivek said. "I mean, no. No mind." Vivek put the black case he was holding to the floor and with one hand, lifted the painting of President Lapin at the stock exchange.

"Sylvester Huppington," Sylvester said to the blank wall. It began to change shape. A massive door started to materialize like a drawing, its rectangular outline appearing line by line, a round, brown knob curving into formation. The knob turned at the touch of Sylvester's finger, and the door slowly opened.

Part II

The Movement

Chapter Eleven: The Art Resistance Movement

You may be shocked by the words you are about to read. If this book reaches the people, you dutiful citizens of The Nation—if it is in fact in your hands, my reader, then I must warn you: None of this is fantasy. These are not the words of a lunatic. Everything you are about to read is true.

Cool air hit my face as I stepped from Sylvester's sunlit office onto the metal, winding stairwell. The handrail sent a quick shiver through me as I circled downward, the light from Sylvester's office vanishing as the door disintegrated overhead. I could hear the soft steps of the person above and below me, as a damp smell reached my nose, and I plunged farther into the darkness. I was beginning to enter into a sort of dizzy haze, when my foot, searching for another step, made me stumble. Two strong arms reached out to stop me from falling. A blue light suddenly zapped, scanning my body from head to toe. It was a good thing I didn't bring any weapons. Then I heard Sylvester's voice say, "Sylvester Huppington," and I watched as a beam of light danced across the veins of an old hand.

The door opened with a loud buzz. We came into a long hallway, and my eyes had to adjust to the lights that hung from the ceiling from wires. The walls were made of limestone rock, wet to the touch. I was hit with an array of scents: the burning of incense, the fresh smell of sawdust, the sweaty odor of bodies. As my vision became clearer, I could make out a man standing beside the entrance, holding a B747 laser pistol. So they did have weapons. The smells were overpowering and I wanted to know where they were coming from; there were probably mind-altering drugs in the air. I would not let myself be manipulated by these creators. They were terrorists, and I had a duty to The Nation. I had to find that weapons facility.

A medley of chants reached my ears and the smell of incense intensified as we walked by an open door on the left. I was awed at what I saw in front of my eyes. The room was nearly the size of a small auditorium, and in one end were men with big bushy beards, black coats, books in their hands, and little hats on their heads. One of them picked up a scroll, carried it around, and kissed it. On another side of the room was a group of bald men, dressed in orange robes, sitting on the ground with their hands together and legs crossed. They were facing a statue of a fat man with a mirthful smile. In another corner of the room were men on small rugs who wore scarves around their heads and murmured in a foreign tongue as they bowed to the ground. In yet another part of the room was a group of both men and women reaching their arms out toward a gigantic computer, chanting. On the computer screen was the number 00001010. In a fifth corner of the room was a group of people with their hands clasped together, peering up at an animated image of an extraterrestrial.

I was never a religious man. But I was brought up Christian like the rest of us, and have found myself immersed in prayer from time to time. I never saw anything like this though. I had heard about people of other religions, of course, but actually seeing them—

their customs were strange to me, yet at the same time compelling. I couldn't stop watching.

And of course there were the faces. Complexions of every hue from yellow to brown to black as night. I knew there were people of other races, but besides the dark metal of the automatrons, the only faces I had ever seen were white.

"We provide white complexion spray so they are not persecuted when they reenter society," Sylvester remarked. "Most of the survivors of the The Purge have taken refuge here. We've taken in more minorities than ever this year since the Cleansing Act."

The door to my right swung open and a man pounced into the hallway. He was shaking, his eyes red and blue, headphones with blaring music hanging off his ears, its cord dangling by his side. He rolled his eyes, his pupils disappearing into his head, and he collapsed to the floor.

"Dear me," Sylvester said. "Vivek, would you carry this iDoser back inside?"

The man pushed himself off the ground with the palms of his hands, and exclaimed, "No need! Ralph has returned!" He stumbled backward, and then caught my eye. I could see an orange tint deep in his pupil.

"Watch," he said. He concentrated hard on what seemed like nothing. And then the outline of a butterfly emerged in the space in front of him. It was yellow, with black lines around its wings, and black spots ran up its back. It flew quickly above my head and around my shoulders, and then it flew *through* me. I shuddered and saw it in the corner of my eye, flying past my ear back to Ralph, who was laughing.

"Can't catch *this* butterfly!" He set his eyes upon it. "Goodbye, my creation." The butterfly evaporated into the air.

"UNICÉ, man!" he said, turning to Lester. "It's taking over our lives, man, our minds … UNICÉ … Thank you Sylvester, you're da biznillidibomb! I'm *transing* hard, man … UNICÉ …" As he said this, his words began to echo "UNICÉ …" and his image faded away, melting into the air, and he was gone.

I had heard the term *'transing'* before. I had *transformed* myself a few times, nothing excessive, mainly into my childhood hero, Detective Conrad. I was no drug addict though like that guy. Anji would use that term in college when she *transformed* into movie stars, something she did too much of. Thank God she stopped all that when she got pregnant. I always thought that UNICÉ was too dangerous for our own good. There were no limitations once inside. You had to be strong to resist its temptations. You couldn't let it take over your mind.

"He disappeared too slowly to be a hologram," Lester commented. "What was he?"

"Some sort of virtual image of the mind, perhaps," Sylvester replied. "I don't spend much time in that room. There's a whole virtual world in there and it's hard to tell what is created and what is reality. The art that can be created through UNICÉ is immense. Half the people in there are on some sort of substance or another. Some of them go onto UNICÉ to escape. Others get lost. There are those who spend weeks inside there, months, even years. They create friends, lovers, and become attached. We've tried to monitor it but it's impossible. The fusion of computers and the human mind is too strong."

I glanced at the door, splashed with paintbrushes that had released a whirlwind of color. What did the door of the weapons facility look like? It had to be somewhere in this hallway.

The next room on the left was smaller than the religion room but just as busy. The sounds of cutting, chiseling, and digitizing filled the air. There was a man sawing a piece of wood and a woman was putting glue on what was going to be the leg of a chair. They worked busily, intensely, and methodically, and when we walked by, they both acknowledged Sylvester.

There were sculptures, made of metal, clay, and ice. I spotted a statuette of a man with a boxy head and muscular physique. Vivek remarked to Iryna, "Who dat man?" She playfully punched him in the chest before drifting over to her sculpture to add some final touches. For a fleeting moment, I imagined myself sculpting Anji.

We walked to the back of the room where ceramists were sitting at their potter's wheels, outlining their designs with fingers in the air. They molded their pots with invisible clay, their eyes darting back and forth as they envisioned their work. When they finished, they strolled to a table where their bowls were printed. One of the potters was drinking water from a mug of his own creation; his initials were inscribed on the bottom. I always thought of cups and bowls as things made by machines in a factory that we used for consumption, and that creating them for the sake of art was something of the past. Yet here was something created as art and it also served a function. If art could be used for practical purposes, could that give it value? I watched one of the potters move his fingers in the air and I found myself wondering what it was he was making.

"Pottery," Sylvester commented, "The oldest art form in the world. You can print anything you'd like here."

The creators were pursuing their own self-gratification. It wasn't just that they were doing something illegal. They had chosen these selfish pursuits instead of dedicating themselves to better jobs where they could provide for their families and enhance the greater good of The Nation.

As I was thinking this, one of the potters stopped working halfway through a bowl to greet Sylvester and show him some of his new glazes. Sylvester listened to the potter with an incredible expression of contentment as his half-shut eyes formed a wrinkly smile. I thought back to what Lauren reminded me: how when I first joined the force, it was because I wanted to make a difference.

When we came back out into the hallway, I could hear grunts and squeals coming from a room on the right. The moaning got louder as we came nearer and Sylvester rolled his eyes, forced to give an explanation.

"Free sex room," he said. "People of any sexual preference forbidden by the government: homosexual, lesbian, bisexual, transsexual, can come here without fear of being imprisoned. We don't discriminate. Multiple partners, S&M, masturbation. Sex suits, sex gowns, they aren't needed in there. Through virtualism, they can create their own fantasies. We insist on periodic STD tests and require an oath of honesty among partners. We don't require contraceptive use, however, and there have been births in there. In fact, we invented pills to counteract the overpopulation preventatives Lapin forces upon us at birth, making it so hard for us to bear fruit. There are so few creators these days. Propagation is imperative for our continued existence."

As we came to another room on the left, a medley of instrumentals floated into the hallway through the open door: the notes of a piano, the strumming of a guitar, the high cacophony of a digital trumpet. When we came inside, the room vibrated with sound as men and women played instruments of every kind. I started to put my hands over my ears, something I had always done since … I didn't want to think about it.

There was a group of young beggars huddled around an acoustic guitar, shouting out lyrics to an unfamiliar song, and I was compelled to listen:

As soon as you're born they make you feel small.
By giving you no time instead of it all.
Till the pain is so big you feel nothing at all.

The young beggars, their eyes closed, bodies swaying, sang with such emotion that I couldn't keep my eyes off them. They spouted out the words as if the whole world needed to hear them.

They hurt you at home and they hit you at school.
They hate you if you're clever and they despise a fool.
Till you're so crazy you can't follow their rules.

When they've tortured and scared you for twenty odd years.
Then they expect you to pick a career.
When you can't really function you're so full of fear.
A working class hero is something to be.

A hero they wanted? That was what they thought of Sylvester.

Keep you doped on religion and sex and TV.
And you think you're so clever and classless and free.
But you're still fucking peasants as far as I can see.

One of the beggars I recognized … the girl with the

notebook! She sang in a high, steady tone, keeping her eyes closed, except when she emphatically chanted, "A working class hero is something to be!" She was too involved in the music to notice me, but I turned my back to her anyway, making a note to avoid looking in her direction on the way out. I had helped her, sure, *as Walter Cunningham*, but I didn't want to take any chances. I faced the other musicians. A woman's fingers waltzed along the keys of a piano, a man rocked along with his saxophone, belting out low, powerful tunes, and a teenager strummed a bass guitar, practicing his chords. As I listened to the notes around me, I had the strange sensation of my body lifting.

I was so distracted by the music that I hardly noticed the scent of paint drifting into my nose. One wall was covered with an enormous canvas. Painters were splashing paint with brushes, and digitizing images from their eyes, into one gigantic array of colors and shapes. I noticed a portrait of Sylvester; a drawing of the Slums; a painting of a waterfall; a photograph of falling leaves. A memory flashed through my mind: sitting on my balcony, looking for the setting sun. Then I thought of Lauren again. What she said. That everyone has a creative side.

And then my brother. What happened as a child. I tried to push it back. Was it a void he was trying to fill?

"Here you are, Lester. The cameras are in the back: still, video, digital. We even have film."

"Thank you so much, Sylvester. But would you mind if I came along for the rest of the tour? I'm just so interested in this place."

I glared at "Marcus Van Dermeen," trying to tell him to stay put, I've got it under control, don't count your automatrons before they breed, and don't blow our cover for God's sake. But he shot me a look back, a quick shifting of the iris to the upper right corner of his eye, saying, I don't want to be left alone with these people, we better stick together.

"All right, Lester," Sylvester replied.

"I play," Vivek said, stomping away into the crowd of musicians. He opened his black case and took out a violin, gently placing the bow along the strings. I could make out the somber Classical sonata, which must have melted Iryna's heart the first time she heard him play.

As we left the room, I could hear the belting voices of the young beggars, chanting,

There's room at the top they are telling you still.
But first you must learn how to smile as you kill.
If you want to be like the folks on the hill.
If you want to be a hero, well, just follow me …

My mind conjured up the strangest image as I left that room. The beggars who were singing were walking behind me, their footsteps following mine, as the guitar continued to strum and their voices reached for my ears. I was leading them out of that room and to the setting sun.

I heard Sylvester close the door, and I shot back to reality. We were nearly reaching the end of the hall. Where was the weapons facility?

There were voices coming from another room on the left. I could hear them through the door. They were aggressive, stormy, and passionate.

"That's the political discussion room," Sylvester said. There was a sign on the door that was written in ink, "Open Forum for All Views." When Sylvester opened the door, I saw a group of people sitting in a circle, arguing. And they were loud.

Two men were in the middle of a debate. One man was

an Upperclassman, with a pointy chin, and unusually long, droopy earlobes. He had a deep, resounding voice. When I first saw him, I thought he was around fifty-years old, but as I walked into the room, and got a closer look at the wrinkles on his forehead and around his eyes, I could see that he was much older.

The other man was in his late twenties. I could tell he was a beggar, covered in dirt from his hair to his coffee-colored socks. He was the less pronounced of the two but he watched Lester and I closely as we entered before continuing the debate.

"Of course. I'm not sayin' I s'port our totalitarian government," the young beggar said. How did he know that term? I had never heard a beggar so educated.

"I would classify The Nation as an 'authoritarian capitalist technocracy,'" corrected the man with the droopy earlobes.

"I know you love big words, Sven, but whatever you wanna call it, I'm not sayin' I s'port it. What I'm sayin' is that a dictatorship is not necessarily a bad thing—dependin' on the leader. If the National Uprising had suh-seeded and Weinstein had taken control, things may 'ave been different."

I cringed at hearing Weinstein's name. It was so rarely spoken in public.

Sven gave a knowing smile. "You see, Simon, there is something you don't know about Lapin. No one does."

"There's somethin' I dunno 'bout the President?"

"That's correct." Sven looked up. "Hello, Syl," he said. I could tell, just by the way Sylvester and Sven looked at each other, that these men had a strong connection.

"Hi, Sven. Just bringing these men on the tour. Fine discussion you're having."

"Yes … indeed." There was silence for a moment.

116

Sylvester was waiting for Sven to continue with the debate but Sven was eyeing us with suspicion, his glassy brown eyes darting back and forth from Lester to me.

"We'll be going then," said Sylvester.

What was it that Sven claimed he knew about President Lapin?

The next door on the right was made of solid granite. I knew in an instant that this must be where the resistance built their weapons, and Sylvester confirmed my suspicions by steering his eyes in the other direction. Next to the door was a voice recognition box with the numbers 0–9 on a panel beside it. I had to get in there somehow. I had to discover that code.

"A blast proof granite door ... what's in *there?*" Lester asked. You had to be kidding me. You don't *ask.*

"That is none of your concern," Sylvester replied quickly, in a sharp tone, and turned his back to us. I gave Lester a long glare.

There were two more doors on the left and right, and at the end of the hall was a door that was inevitably an escape exit, which I figured led to the paper book archive and then out to the street.

"Here," Sylvester said to me as we reached the last door on the left, "is where the writers meet." I looked at the door, its white paint peeling, an old-fashioned doorknob that turned. "But writer's workshop does not meet for a few minutes. Come this way. There's something important that all new members must see." He led us into the last room on the right. "Besides our archive, here are the last remaining paper books in The Nation. These books," he said with a pause, "were written from the heart. This is the reading room."

I had never heard a silence so loud. The only audible sound was the occasional turning of a page. Books lined the shelves and rested on tables. The air had a calm, antiquated smell—the musty scent of yellowy pages of stories growing old. People were sitting on couches and chairs, paper books in their hands. From what I could tell, no one was on UNICÉ.

Sylvester led us inside. He motioned to the shelves. I hesitated for a moment and then walked by the stacks of books with Lester behind me. I hadn't seen paper books since I was a child. I scanned the titles, touching the edges of the pages with my fingers. I came to one book that was coming apart, its cover about to fall to the ground. I found myself taking the book out and putting the pages back into the cover. I glanced at the title: *The Great Gatsby* by F. Scott Fitzgerald.

Sylvester smiled at me from the doorway. He pointed to an auburn, leather couch in the center of the room. When I sank into it, I felt like I could spend days just sitting there. Sylvester came up to us and took out a small sheet of parchment. He tucked it into my jacket pocket, leaned his head toward mine, and whispered in my ear, "For later."

"That ends the tour," Sylvester said to us both. "You're welcome to pick a book off the shelf." He walked out of the reading room and back into the hallway. I watched as Iryna came up to him and they talked quietly together. I couldn't hear them, but I saw Sylvester motion with his hand toward us and then close the door.

Chapter Twelve: Writer's Workshop

Lester gave me a soft nudge with his elbow, put a book in front of his face, and looked into the lens of his glasses. I looked around at the other people in the room—they were engrossed in their reading—and I picked up a book from the table beside me, lifted it to my face and went onto UNICÉ.

"We've got to get a picture of the weapons facility," Lester said.

"A picture?" I asked. "What would that do? We have to get inside and get some physical evidence."

"How?"

"By gaining their trust."

"These people are freaking me out. I want to do something now."

"Don't be a fool! The time isn't right. It takes time to gain someone's trust. Eventually, they'll be opening that door for us. Sit tight. And no more going on UNICÉ. It's too suspicious."

"So you're just gonna sit here then?"

"I'm going to read."

I took off my glasses. One of the readers was watching us. I closed the book that was covering my face and was about to get up and walk to the bookshelf when I glanced down at the dark, rusty cover of the book I was holding. *An Autobiography: My Life and the*

Creation of ARM by Sylvester Huppington. Interesting.

Lester was just sitting there, so I placed the book on the couch and scanned the shelves for a book for him. I pulled one out with a bright orange cover and a title in big white letters: *One Fish, Two Fish* by Dr. Seuss. Perfect.

I sunk back into the couch, placing Sylvester's book on my lap. I handed Lester the book I chose for him, and remarked, "This looks like something you'd like."

He stared at the cover, confused. "This is retarded," he whispered out loud. Two of the readers looked in our direction. He rolled his eyes and turned to the first page.

I looked down at Sylvester's book. It was heavy. 250 pages. Wow. He wrote this whole thing. I had to admit, in a strange way, I found myself admiring Sylvester. I couldn't imagine what it would take to write an entire book. This was the kind of man who could lead a resistance movement.

Lester looked down at *One Fish, Two Fish* and shook his head. Then he stood. Eyes from other readers lifted from their books and stared at us. He walked out of the room.

I thought about stopping him. Making up some story on the spot to convince him to sit back down. I was even tempted to go after him into the hallway. But I had warned Lester to stay put, *ordered* him to do nothing, and he was a fool. If he did something dumb, I wouldn't be there with him.

I had to know what writer's workshop entailed. I pulled out the piece of parchment that Sylvester tucked into my pocket. The words were written in silver. I read:

Five Rules of Writer's Workshop:
1. No communication with each other outside of ARM.
2. Never come to WW as a hologram.
3. Never write anything on UNICÉ. Write everything by hand.
4. Come to WW with writing, or a writer's plan.
5. You must share your writing with the other members.

I looked up to see Sylvester's old round head leaning through the crack of the door of the reading room. "It's time," he said. I put Sylvester's autobiography aside. I'd read it later.

The writer's workshop room was filled with a singular, circular table in the center of the room. There were fifteen chairs and fourteen of them were filled. Every writer had a notebook and something to write with, laid out on the table in front of them in a perfectly set manner. They sat erect in their chairs, calm as can be, watching me as I sat down. The beggar girl with the notebook wouldn't stop looking at me. "I know you!" she cried out. "You helped me!" Looking at her torn clothes, and taking in her ratty scent, I felt a mixture of surprise and interest. She was a beggar, and here I was, sitting at the same table with her, as an equal.

"This man defended me 'gainst a policeman!" she exclaimed, looping a strand of curly hair with her finger. The young man next to her—Simon, from the political debate—nodded his head at me. He was holding the girl's hand.

Sylvester smiled favorably in my direction from the head of the table. "This man writes for a living, Sara," he said in response to the girl, but addressing all the writers. "He's a news reporter."

"A reporter?" asked a snarling voice.

I looked around the table. The man who had spoken was Sven, the man with the droopy earlobes from the political discussion room, the man who claimed he knew something about President Lapin that no one else did.

"I didn't know that there were still news reporters," he said, eyeing me. "I thought everyone got their news from the newsman."

"There's still the People's News, the last running celebrity magazine in The Nation," I replied.

"Spam, you mean?"

"Sven, let's ..." Sylvester interrupted, "move on with writer's workshop. Walter, our newest member, is a news reporter. But he wears a disguise."

I knew it. My suspicions, his kindness, requesting me for an interview, this was the moment Sylvester was waiting for. To expose me in front of the writers.

"In truth, he is a poet, who has been searching for a place to share his thoughts and emotions. Welcome, Walter Cunningham, to our community of writers."

"Welcome, Walter," everyone said in unison. Sharing thoughts and emotions? These creators were kind of weirding me out.

"What's happenin' with the *trial*, Sylvestuh?" Sara asked, her eyes widening with curiosity.

"It's in the hands of the lawyers now."

I gulped.

"Even if we lose and the book archive is closed," Sylvester continued, "we've still got ARM, and we've still got the reading room. They don't know about *that*. Now, let us begin. We always offer new members of writer's workshop the opportunity to share their works when they first join, since we know the pain of having so much to say but no one to listen. Walter, would you like to share one of your poems?"

I was dreading this moment. I wished I could somehow evade it. Reason told me to read what I had written. But all I could think about were the fourteen pairs of eyes looking in my direction.

"Is it okay if I read next time?"

Sylvester cleared his throat. "Did you have a chance to read the five rules of writer's workshop?"

"Yes, I did."

"Well, the fifth rule, as you recall, is that you must share your writing with other members of the workshop."

"Of course ... but I'd rather share next time, if that's okay. I'd like to see how everyone else does it first."

"All right, Walter, I understand. Since this is your first time here. It is for everyone to receive feedback in order to improve our writing."

I tried to force a smile. But the thought of my poem being examined by other eyes, words being crossed out with red ink, other minds pushing themselves into mine—made me want to get the hell out of there. Yet at the same time, I was strangely compelled to writer's workshop. I hadn't even looked at the time until forty minutes had passed and writer's workshop was over. The writings were sad, happy, angry, funny, romantic: they were filled with emotion. They were *genuine*. As Sylvester said, they came from the heart. That was what Walter Cunningham had to write before returning to ARM. And he still didn't know how.

"All right, everyone," Sylvester said. "That wraps up writer's workshop for to— "

Sylvester was interrupted by a gasp coming from the hallway.

And then a shot rang out. I jumped out of my seat and rushed out of the room. There was a crowd of people in the hallway. Some were clutching instruments tightly against their chest, some held paintbrushes dripping with fresh paint, others were naked except for towels around their waists. I pushed through them. There, lying in front of the solid granite door was Lester. Behind him, with a laser pistol emitting blue rays into the air, was Iryna Huppington.

"This man was trying to get inside the weapons facility!" Iryna shouted, with a hint of uncertainty in her wavering voice. She fished through Lester's pockets and pulled out the photographs of pigeons. "He claims he's a photographer," she said. "Does this look like art to you?"

"Pardon me!" The crowd moved aside so that Sylvester could walk through. "Oh God, Iryna. You didn't need to kill him."

"Let me handle it, Dad."

"Let me assure you," he said, speaking to the crowd. "This man was an informant. We know this because a fellow creator, who I will not reveal for this person's safety, tipped us off. Now please, everyone, go back to your rooms."

"This is what happens to rats!" Iryna shouted.

"How many times have I told you to refrain from violence?" Sylvester scolded, a hint of sadness in his eyes.

"If you keep interfering like this, I won't ever be able to lead."

At that moment, Iryna's hazel eyes landed on me. "Walter Cunningham. You verified this man, did you not?"

I didn't respond. I was looking down in horror. "I can't believe he's dead ..." I muttered.

"Oh, cut the crap!" Iryna exclaimed. "Did you verify him or not?"

"Yes."

The creators shifted their gaze from Iryna to me. Iryna pointed the laser pistol at my chest. "Well then? What do you have to say for yourself?"

"It's clear what happened."

"Nothing is clear at the moment except that there is a gun pointing at you."

"The man is a detective, and a sloppy one at that," I continued. "He went undercover, pretending to be my banker so that I could verify him when this day came."

"Put down the gun, Iryna," Sylvester said. "He's one of us."

"You're not going to shoot me," I said to her. "I can see it in your eyes."

Behind that tough exterior, beneath her rebellious spirit, I could see in those hazel eyes of hers that shooting me was but an idle threat. She hadn't even reenergized her laser beams. She was incensed. It was as if the rays of the gun had risen from her head in bursts of steam. But her arm dropped to her side, and with it the gun that had killed Lester, and I could have sworn that I saw, trapped beneath her iris and the lens of her eye, a small veil of water.

"All right, everyone, the show is over," Sylvester said, looking down disgustedly at Lester. The creators began to disperse, peering over their shoulder as Vivek dragged the body away. I didn't move. My eyes were glued to Lester's corpse, wondering why it wasn't me.

✵

Writing or a writer's plan. There I was, sitting at my desk with a pad and pen, and once again, I didn't know where to begin. I needed Lauren. And there was only one place she could be.

125

"Lauren McQuade on UNICÉ."

"Hey Victor! I'll be at your office in a flash."

Why did she want to meet me here? I told the door to lock. If Anji came in again it would be bad news.

Lauren's hologram appeared. When she saw me, she smiled, and watched my eyes as they rested on a fake, holographic detective badge that was pinned to the front pocket of her cop uniform, over her right breast.

"Remember it?" she asked, bouncing up and down. "That's the badge we made together!"

"Yeah … I remember."

"I'm just glad things went okay at ARM … they did, right? How did the poem go over?"

"Fine. And how did you know it was called ARM?"

Lauren's cheery expression vanished and she was as still and serious as an automatron.

"Just admit it, Lauren, that you were the one who tipped off The Chief. It will make things a lot easier."

"I'll admit nothing until *you* admit that you've realized that there are a lot of messed up things going on. You saw the creators. They're not slaves to consumerism like the rest of us. If only they could somehow overthrow Lapin, they could set things right."

"What you're saying is treason, Lauren."

She didn't hear me. She was looking past me and when I glanced behind my shoulder, I realized that she wasn't looking at anything at all. It was then that I first noticed an orange tint deep within her pupils from overuse of UNICÉ. She was wearing an expression of horror, as if she were reliving a nightmare. When she spoke, it sounded as if she were possessed.

"It was me. I told The Chief. I turned them in. I'll never know how to live with myself. Guilt. It takes over a person and never lets them go." She looked at me suddenly, saying, "Forgive me."

I felt myself taking a step back, away from her. "Lauren ... you're acting crazy."

"I told Sylvester about Lester. Not about you, Victor. It was the only way I could make amends ... Did you see the beauty in art?"

"Jeeze, Lauren, I didn't realize you were so affected by the creators—"

"Did you see it, Victor? Tell me you saw it."

These weird, sudden shifts in emotion scared the shit out of me. I knew Lauren was undercover at ARM. But these feelings of guilt, her eerie cheerfulness—the creators must have put her under a spell of some kind. I had better just tell her what she wanted to hear.

So I looked into her eyes, and said, "I saw it."

"And Sylvester? You know he is a great man?"

"Yes, I liked him."

She smiled. "I knew you would."

I looked away. "I have a job to do though. And I still can't write. I need you to help me."

"You'll come up with something."

"Well, I ... don't know where to start. I really need your help with this. Do you know of any other techniques like the one from before?"

"Tap into your creative side, Victor. I know you have it in you."

"I don't know what I'm doing!" I was getting aggravated. "And I have to come to writer's workshop with some writing, or at least a writer's plan."

"I believe in you. I always felt like I really connected with you, more than any other man."

"What?"

"You don't feel like we connect?"

"No, I do," I said, looking down at my empty pad. "I feel a connection too."

"And I never understood," she said, looking at Anji's picture, "how such an accomplished lawyer—the daughter of Dallas Grumm—could care so much about trivial things like shoes … how she could be so shallow. I never understood what you saw in her." Then she added under her breath, "I guess she always did have *money*."

Something inside me snapped. She had no right to talk about Anji that way.

"Get out of my office! Go back to your life as a slave to UNICÉ. You're not helping me write. So you're of no use to me."

We froze for a moment and it felt like time had stopped. Lauren's eyes looked glossed over but she didn't cry. She didn't make a sound. We were both stunned into silence.

Finally, Lauren uttered in a small voice, "Return," and vanished.

Chapter Thirteen: Like Father, Like Son

Tommy batted third on his blockball team. He had impressed his coach in tryouts, hitting the football consistently with the rectangular bat I bought him for his birthday last year. Although Tommy was short, he was speedy, and could avoid the tacklers and safeties to run successful touchdowns before the pitcher was able to run the ball to the end zone. Tommy loved to hit the ball down the right side of the field.

Anji and I sat in the back row of the stands. I noticed a man who held a package in his arms and was wearing a hooded jacket that concealed his face. I wasn't about to take my eyes off this shady character for the rest of the game, but maybe I was just being paranoid.

Across the aisle from us was a woman who had actually brought her nanokit to the game. She tried to hide the needle under her coat but it was obvious and disgusting—*transforming* in public! I nudged Anji on the shoulder and pointed at the woman. Then Tommy's team came onto the field. I spotted Tommy in the dugout and turned to Anji. She didn't see him. She was still watching the woman *transform*.

The game began but it was hard for me to pay attention. I couldn't stop thinking about the case. Why didn't Iryna shoot me after killing Lester? Why did Vivek say he knew me? Did Sylvester really believe I was a creator? For some reason, these people wanted me to join their movement; Sylvester requested me for an interview in the first place. I couldn't help but think that they were using me in some way. Maybe they knew that I was married to Anji and they didn't want to kill their attorney's husband while she defended them and then once the trial was over, they'd kill us both.

Charlie, the team's pitcher, whose spiky hair I could see from the stands, snickered the first time Anji shouted Tommy's name. Snickering was all Charlie was capable of—he couldn't throw a single strike and was taken out of the game in the second inning. Tommy pretended he didn't hear Anji, but when his mother shouted his name, I could see a smile forming under the rim of his helmet.

He struck out three times. But at the end of the game, when it mattered most, Tommy scored a touchdown. He hit the ball to the right side of the field and ran as fast as his little legs could carry him, his teammates blocking the defensive line from tackling into him. He beat the pitcher to the end zone and turned to see his teammates jumping up and down from the dugout. The light of The Guardian shined brighter than ever, illuminating the field in its white glow.

Anji and I walked down to the field. I spotted Amber, accompanied by her friends, trotting there as well, her purple pigtails slapping against her back as she skipped every other step on the way down. The players formed two lines and shook hands. I watched as Tommy came to Charlie and offered him his hand. Only a few feet from them, we heard Tommy say, "Good game."

"What do you got, a corked bat?"

"Huh? Just because you couldn't throw a strike doesn't mean everyone else cheated," Tommy replied.

"I just thought," Charlie said, "you know the phrase,

'like father like son'? Well, maybe it should be, 'like grandfather, like grandson.'"

Anji's eyes widened when Charlie said that. She wanted to rush across the field to Tommy, but I put my hand on her arm, saying, "Let him fight his own battles."

"What are you talking about?" Tommy asked. "My grandfather never cheated."

"I bet your *mom* never told you he 'tampered with evidence'! That's what I heard!" Charlie looked past me, into the stands. I turned around, and there, sitting at the top of the stands, was the hooded man, and I could finally make out the features of his face. Kenneth.

How did he escape the TPF? Kenneth lifted the package so that Charlie could see it, revealing a box shaped like a liquidator. Only one videotron came in a box like that: "Richard Pellman: Virtual Fight 12."

I wanted to choke him. How dare he mess with my family? Bribing a kid to antagonize my son! But before I could do anything, Charlie, with a glint in his eye after seeing the videogame, turned back to Tommy, and shouted, "Your grandfather is a cheat, your father can't make any money, and your portrait sucked!" He turned and began walking away.

Tommy pushed him to the ground. I saw Amber gazing at Tommy with admiration.

Charlie got into Tommy's face, egging him on, "You gonna push me from behind, but you're too afraid to hit me from the front, huh? Come on, I bet you're too scared to hit me with your *mom* here and without your *dad* to fight your battles for you! I dare you—hit me!"

I watched as Tommy tightened his hand into a fist, then pulled his arm back, and hit Charlie smack in the face. Charlie collapsed to the ground, his head inches from the end zone. He didn't get up.

❧

When I got home, I immediately went onto UNICÉ.

"Send message to Kenneth Fletcher," I said. "Meet me in the cubes room."

"Kenneth Fletcher is on UNICÉ."

As I entered the room, so did Kenneth, wearing that mischievous grin.

"You always told me, Kenneth, the first rule of detectives is not to mix work with family."

"Take back what you said to The Chief."

"You know I can't do that."

"Why *not*?"

"You better get into hiding, Kenneth, before the TPF find you."

Kenneth chuckled insolently. "You really think I escaped, Victor? They let me out. I have a friend in the TPF, remember? Connections are the most important things if you want to move up in this world. Don't burn bridges. You'll never know when you'll need to cross over them again."

"Thanks for the lesson," I said sarcastically. I found myself thinking back to the days when Kenneth taught me how to be a detective. I never sought out my real father during those years. "You know, Kenneth, *you* betrayed *me*. I used to look up to you. But you made me lie for you so many times … and then you shot that beggar."

Kenneth paused for a moment. He seemed lost in thought, his eyes gazing at the cubes, still in their chaotic positions from a previous game and ready to be put back in their proper places. In that gaze I could see the old Kenneth, who loved his wife deeply, who worked hard, and who cared about what I thought. And then he commented, with a hint of resignation in his voice, "Just take back what you said to The Chief and I'll leave your family alone."

"I can't do it. Never."

"Yes, you can!" Kenneth jumped out of his seat. His fury had returned. He hurled the cubes at me. They swirled in different directions. I heard one whiz by my ear and felt another zip through my chest. I shuddered.

"I oughtta kill you!" he shouted.

"Why don't you?"

"It's too *good* for you. I want you kicked off the force. An eye for an eye. That's justice."

I felt like killing him. I would be protecting my family, as a lion protects his cubs. But I'm not as foolish or impulsive as Kenneth. So instead, I said calmly, but firmly, "Stay away from me and my family if you know what's good for you. And get your life together." I left the cubes room, and messaged The Chief. He promised me he'd take care of it. That the TPF would make Kenneth disappear for good if he threatened my family or me again. I was too important to the TPF, as long as I was on this case. They needed me. They wouldn't let anyone kill me, as long as I was helping them bring down the creators.

I went into my bedroom and lied down on top of the satin sheets while Anji brushed her hair. Even if I did believe The Chief that the TPF wouldn't let Kenneth hurt us, Kenneth was now free. If Kenneth would go to such lengths as to befriend Charlie to get at my son, what else would he do to bring me down? I didn't want to think about it because I knew Kenneth and he was a plotter. He'd hide things from me during cases and suddenly act, fulfilling a plan that he had mulled over in his head a thousand times, and I had to follow him blindly. I felt the same way as I did then. I still couldn't see.

Yet I didn't believe that Kenneth was my biggest

threat. If the creators found out I was a detective, they'd kill me. I saw what they did to Lester. Kenneth, on the other hand, had murdered, but it was always in the name of the law, despite the times he pointed guns at people. He killed out of duty to The Nation, in that corrupted mind of his. So besides him interfering with Tommy (who I was proud of, by the way, for defending himself, and giving that boy a concussion), I wasn't as concerned with Kenneth as I was about the creators.

I assured my wife though, as she pulled the knots from her thick curls at the table in our bedroom, that she and Tommy were safe. As I gazed at the curve of her back, I could tell by her silent reply that she longed for me to tell her the details of the case; we had always discussed our work before. I knew this was straining our relationship, but I had to protect her. She had still not forgiven me for leaving her at The Mountain Theater.

Anji began humming an exaggeratedly joyful tune.

"What's that song?" I asked her, attempting to engage her somehow.

"The theme song from the new Kelly Karr movie." She crumpled her nose as she worked at another knot. Anji always looked pained trying to smooth out her hair. I bought her an electronic hairbrush for her birthday, but she never used it. It was if she enjoyed the struggle with the tangles—the challenge. As if brushing her hair was an extension of being a lawyer— the fighter in Anji. Sometimes I thought of Anji as an 'all or nothing' type of person (and I think I'm the same way), which is what's made her so successful at her job. I always thought the other areas of Anji's life were there to compensate for the stress and high energy of her work. Either that or they were escapes. There was her obsession with shoes, for example. The meticulous designing of our house. The way she adhered to her "Qi," which she believed was good for keeping a sense of order in the home.

Then there was how and when she wanted to have sex. I couldn't believe how often she wanted to do it in college, what she'd want to do. She got turned on when I came to her as a hologram and we used transmission sensation devices. It was great for me; she was my first and it felt like I was making up for lost time. For her, it was great too. It was as if I were a vehicle for her to escape her sheltered youth. From her *father*. When she started working for him though, sex became more of a routine. She even called it a "de-stressor" once under her breath. She'd always want to do it the night before a big trial. I lost some of my passion too. It was wrong. We were in our early thirties. And we weren't making love. Then again, Anji had always used her sex gown and me my sex suit; so maybe, we had never really made love at all.

And we weren't expressing it in words either. She wouldn't say "I love you" without me saying it first. I knew she still loved me, of course, but it'd still be nice to hear her say those three words to me every once in a while.

Then there were the movies and television. Instead of doing it, Anji would lie in bed and watch movies on UNICÉ. She admitted that it was an escape. What really bothered me was the way she watched them. Once late at night, when she thought I was sleeping, I snuck a peek at her face. Her lips were moving; she was mouthing the lines from the movie. She wasn't there with me. Her eyes were glossed over in a look of strange nostalgia, her presence lost in an imaginary world.

I liked to tease her about the brush. "So you're still

not using the electronic brush? You know, that was the most expensive item in the hair products section of virtual shopping!"

She shot me a look through the mirror. "You know, you really do spoil me."

In college, Anji had everything a girl could want: the nicest brands of pocketbooks and shoes, the newest mini-automatron, even her own flying car. I knew Anji was used to nice things, and if I were going to marry her, I'd have to adjust to that. But I liked giving Anji stuff. I just wanted her to be happy.

My parents rarely paid me attention. Unless the silent treatment counts.

"How's the trial going?" It amazed me how our lives seemed so separate while they were so inextricably intertwined.

"Why should I tell you?" she snapped. Then she uttered under her breath, "You don't talk about your work."

Uh oh. "Anji, come here." She kept brushing. "Anji. Come to bed."

"Hold on." She put the brush down and got up from the table, checking the doors to make sure they were closed, and going to her closet. "Bar," she said, and the gold bar shot out of the wall, her sexsuit and sleepsuit hanging beside each other. She took off her suit and tie and slipped on her sleepsuit. She looked innocent in that one-piece pink outfit. She walked to her side of the bed, got under the sheets, and looked at me. It killed me the way her caramel eyes gazed tenderly into mine, two strands of hair outlining her face in soft, sweet curves. One strand fell haphazardly across her cheek as she rested her head on the pillow. She tried to pull back the strand but I held her wrist gently with my hand. "No," I said. "Keep it just like that." I put my arm around her.

"You know why I can't talk about work. It's for your own safety."

Anji's eyes searched mine. "I understand. Just … be careful, okay?"

"I will. How's the trial?"

"Tiring."

"What's it like working with Sylvester Huppington?"

"Oh, I don't see him. I meet with someone named Sven."

Sven! Sylvester trusted him enough to represent his company…

"Well, babe, all you can do is your best."

"No." She turned her back to me. I let my arm fall around her waist. "I need to win. For Dad. To prove to the world that he was an honest man."

"Well, you'll win then. The Nation will do what's right." As I spoke those words, they felt forced, not fully meaning them anymore. A twinge of anxiety unsettled my stomach.

She turned on her back. "I'm glad that kid, Charlie, is okay. Where did Tommy learn how to punch like that?" she asked with a wink.

"All right, maybe I taught him a few things. Sometimes I don't know, Anji. I'm afraid we spoil him too much."

"Just as you spoil me?"

"I'm serious."

I wish I had an example—someone I could learn from, who knew how to raise a son. There was my adoptive father to show me what *not* to do. And then my real father—well, he did teach me *something*. To never abandon a child.

"Did you see that girl with the purple pigtails come up to Tommy after what happened?" Anji asked. "She likes him."

"Yeah, Amber. He asked her out."

"Really? He told you that?"

"Yep. She said 'no' though."

"Well, at least he asked her out," she said. She twisted her knuckles into my arm. "It's more than you did with me!"

"More than I did, huh?" I said, getting on top of her. "I'll show you what I can do!" I went to kiss her but she stopped me.

"What are you doing?" she asked. "I don't have my sex gown on."

I thought about how we kissed so passionately in my office before we went to The Mountain Theater. Maybe we could rekindle that flame. We could make love. So I asked, "what if we tried without it?"

She searched my eyes for a moment. Then she responded, "That's impossible."

"Fine," I said, rolling back onto my side of the bed.

Chapter Fourteen: The TPF

The Chief had recently gotten a haircut. His dark hair was buzzed in a perfect circle so that bangs fell from his forehead around to the back of his head. Many of the most fashionable celebrities were flaunting their bowl cuts. The Chief was always one of the first to take on the hippest trends, particularly when it pertained to his appearance.

When I came into The Chief's office, there were self-administered diagnostic kits haphazardly placed on his desk. There was one for detecting signs of heart disease, one for preventing cancer, and one for curing diabetes. The Chief removed the diabetes tube from his mouth as I took a seat in front of his desk, asking, "What are ya looking at?"

"Nothing ... just here for the meeting."

"I'm the one who asks the questions round here."

"I didn't ask a question—"

"I don't need to explain myself. I'll talk to you if I feel like it." He paused. "And I feel like it. The reason for all these kits goes back to one of my famous quotes. As I always say, 'better safe than sorry.'"

"I've never heard you say that, Chief."

"Don't be a smart ass! You better take down those creators, Vale. I'm going to live to see the day that vengeance is taken for what they did to my son." He looked over at his son's comb and his face reddened, before looking back at me. "And you, Vale, are going to do it. Do you understand?"

"I'll take down the creators. You have my word on that. But by putting Lester on this case, you exposed me. I stuck out my neck for him and it almost got me killed. I want to work alone."

The Chief looked at me hard. Then he leaned back in his chair and his mustache twitched. "Sure, Victor. I wouldn't want to expose you. I always protect my officers."

The loud whir of a TPF helicopter came down from the sky and took control of the room. I covered my hands with my ears, something I did when I heard that sound. Ever since what happened to my brother.

I hated the technological police. To get where they were, they knew someone, paid someone, fucked someone. The TPF were the only ones allowed to leave The City, on their helicopters and planes. But the price they paid for their power was fatal. At the slightest mistake, they would disappear, their names eradicated from UNICÉ.

The resounding thuds of their midnight-black boots increased as they came closer to The Chief's office. Everything they wore was black: their leather hats, puffy nanojackets, gloves, baggy pants. Their belts held liquidators, missile guns, deactivators, mirror-reflective shields, electronic handcuffs. Their large, black-rimmed goggles could transmit messages directly to the President's quarters. These goggles were the only devices I ever saw them use, or pretend to. Their accessories were excessive. Lapin did not equip the TPF officers with these advanced weapons so that they could be used. She may have believed that, but I knew it wasn't so. Lapin thought she was invoking fear among the masses—and by God, she was—but she was the one who was the most afraid. She couldn't stand the thought of losing power.

The door swung open so hard that it nearly popped out of its hinges. Five TPF officers marched into the office as if it were their own. And by all practical means, it was.

"Call in your detective, Victor Vale," said the officer who had led them inside.

"He is here," replied The Chief, pointing to me.

"Good, good," the TPF officer replied, looking me over through his goggles. The man's eyes were as dark as his clothes and his lips barely parted when he spoke. He walked over to The Chief's razor selection and snatched one with his hand, causing the shelf to shake. Three razors fell to the ground, along with the comb. I saw The Chief's eyes linger on his son's comb, which landed a few feet from his chair. He didn't dare pick it up.

The officer looked into the mirror and began shaving off the stubble on his chin. "I saw a policewoman when I came in," he said as he shaved. "Blonde. With big tits."

Fear struck through me. What did he want with Lauren?

"I'm thirsty. Send her in with some tea."

"Well, that's usually the job of our automatron. Officers come to the station in person once a month for security—"

The officer stopped shaving and dropped the razor to the ground. It shattered, its pieces crawling like insects away from the officer in different directions.

The Chief spoke into his desk, "Officer McQuade to my office please. And with some … tea. For the gentleman here."

The officer picked up another razor and continued to shave off his stubble while gazing into the mirror. "Now, Detective. You've been investigating the local terrorists. Is it true that Sylvester Huppington is hiding a community of creators beneath Huppington Books™? The man has been a great supporter of the President in the past, so know your facts before answering."

"Yes, it's true."

"You've been inside?"

"Yes."

The officer checked himself in the mirror one last time and dropped the razor back onto the shelf. He came to where I was sitting and looked me directly in the eye.

"Are they planning a terrorist plot against The Nation?"

"I don't know, officer."

He was so close to my face that I could smell the freshness of his recently shaved chin. His dark irises peered into mine.

"Where are they located?"

"In an underground lair beneath Huppington Books™. The entrance is in Sylvester Huppington's office, behind a painting. Voice recognition and hand activation are required."

"And the weapons facility? How do we get in there?"

"There is a code."

"Yes, I know there is a code! What is it?"

"I don't know but I'll find out."

"Why did Sylvester Huppington request you for an interview?"

"I don't know."

"You don't know much, do you?"

"In time, I'll find out."

He searched my eyes once more and then backed

away, saying, "You are a smart one, detective."

Lauren walked in, carrying a tray with a teapot and two glasses of tea. She did a double take when she realized that it was me who was sitting there. She was wearing her cop uniform, the tight blue pants and button-down shirt. She also wore the small, silver earrings that her grandmother had passed down to her.

When the officer heard the glasses clinking against the teapot, he turned, looked at her, and smiled.

"Nice earrings," the TPF officer said in an overly complimentary tone, pointing to her grandmother's small, silver hoops.

"Thank you," she replied, a bit surprised. "I got them from-"

"How superficial are women?" the officer said to The Chief, ignoring her. "With their diamond rings, their pocketbooks, their shoes." As he said this, he was leering at Lauren's breasts.

Lauren looked up at The Chief for some sort of signal. When he didn't give it, she started walking toward his desk to put down the tray, but the TPF officer put out his hand.

"What's your name?"

"Officer McQuade."

He took a step toward her.

"Your *first* name."

"Lauren."

"Lauuuren," he said, coming closer, the only thing between them the tray of tea. "Why don't you put that tea down and go up to the roof and I'll take you for a ride in my helicopter." He put one hand on her cheek, and with the other, he undid the top button of her shirt.

"Don't touch me!" Lauren yelled. She rushed to the door but one of the other TPF officers grabbed her from behind.

"Now, now," said the TPF officer. "Let men be men. You'll never be as powerful as us."

Lauren laughed.

"And why are you *laughing*?"

"The president of The Nation—who you take orders from—is a woman. With UNICÉ, force no longer brings power. What you need is a shrewd head. The brain of a woman."

He came toward her again, his face inches from hers. "I'll teach you a thing or two about force and power." He began to play with a strand of her hair. Then put a hand around her neck. "I suggest you make this easy on yourself."

Lauren's eyes shifted to me. "Victor!!" she screamed. "Help me!"

I looked up at the portrait of Detective Conrad that hung behind The Chief's desk. He would have helped Lauren. He defended the common people from the TPF.

I got out of my chair. The TPF officer turned to look at me, daring me with his eyes to challenge him. I stared back at him and said, "Don't lay a hand on her."

I took a step forward. One of the TPF officers rushed at me and I socked him in the face. Then three of them ran at me. I managed to hit another but one of them kicked me in the stomach and then the other grabbed me from behind. I turned my head to look at The Chief. He couldn't even meet my eye.

"Who do you think you *are*?" the TPF officer asked, approaching me. "Some hot shot detective because you've been given this case? Well, you're just a poster boy. So the police department is happy. What you do means *nothing*."

"Not true," I said. "Sylvester requested me—he likes me, for whatever reason. I'm the only one who can gain his trust and get you access to the weapons facility."

He glared at me with those dark eyes and curled his lip so it nearly reached the tip of his nose. He looked like he was about to explode. But all he did was kick me in the groin. I fell to the ground. He eyed Lauren and licked his lips.

"How can you do this?" Lauren asked. "Don't you have any morals?"

The officer laughed. "Morals?" He looked down at me, gave me a pat on the back, and said, as if passing on friendly advice, "There is no purpose for morals when you have power." I lifted my head and watched his black, leather boots pounding against the floor as he walked toward Lauren, saying,

"Now put down that tea and come with me."

The tray shook as she placed it on The Chief's desk. She couldn't look at me. The TPF officer smacked her in the ass with the palm of his hand and she hurried out of the room with a cry of surprise. He laughed at the noise and took a long sip of tea before dropping it abruptly on the tray.

"Ew. No sugar."

He motioned to the other officers. "Let's get outta here." When they let go of me, I was tempted to go after them. To save Lauren. But there was nothing more I could do. The TPF officer walked to the open doorway. Then he turned and faced me, glaring into my eyes.

"I know who you are, Detective Vale, and if you try to pull a stunt like that again," he said, adding matter-of-factly, "I wouldn't mind adding the daughter of Dallas Grumm to my list."

✎

I was above her. The hormones released, sweat from my brow falling onto the pillow. Sex gowns wrapped around our bodies; the blue meshed with the red into a single color. I looked into my wife's face. But I didn't see Anji. Her hair was lighter, her eyes blue. Her moans of pleasure were shrieks of pain. I was seeing Lauren's face and I—

I was looking at her through goggles as the whirring of a helicopter soared through the night.

I awoke. Gusts of breath blew the strands of hair that covered Anji's face as she slept. I walked out to the balcony and listened to the stillness in the air. I looked at the tomatoes, the cucumbers, the lilacs, which were dark in the shadow of the sky. We couldn't eat these vegetables. There was no pollen in these flowers.

I gazed across at The Mountain. Thought about the girl in the elevator who had seen a whale. She had no reason to ever leave that place.

I looked up at The Guardian and realized for the first time that it wasn't protecting us. It was preventing us from getting out.

I came back to the bedroom. I put my mouth to the chestnut curls around her ear. I whispered, "We're powerless, Anji. I thought it was our job to protect the people. But we can't even protect each other."

I got dressed quickly and went into my office. Shot the needle in a fresh vein. Leaned forward in the maroon chair. Looked into the empty sky. "Lauren? Are you there?"

"Yes, Victor." The softness of her voice and nothing else.

"Cubes?"

A chuckle. Then silence.

146

"Are you okay?"

"What do you think?"

I fought against my mind not to imagine what Lauren looked like … what was done to her.

"I'm going to report this."

"To who? *We're* the police."

"It doesn't matter. I'll tell The Chief to—"

"The Chief won't do anything and you know it."

I stared into the cloudy sky, past the Kelly Karr Moldable Shoes™ that click-clacked and the Elena Perfume™ that sprayed its sweet nectarine scent into the air.

"Victor?" Her voice was a little higher.

"Yes?"

"I've been sad." There was a crack in her voice, as if it took great strength to push out those words. "But now, I'm not sad anymore. I'm broken."

"It'll be better. I promise."

"No, it won't. Nothing will ever be the same."

"I'm sorry, Lauren. I didn't mean those things I said."

"It's okay. I forgive you. You've done what you could for me."

"I really do feel a connection to you. You're my best friend. But Anji is my wife. I love her. Nothing can change that."

"I understand." Her voice cracked.

Silence.

"I want to leave this world. Go across the sea," she said.

"But you can't."

I didn't want to give her false hope. But I found myself looking hard into the clouds of the sky of UNICÉ, wanting to push them apart to see what was there. I lowered my gaze to the tops of my kneecaps. Our world was all we knew. Shouldn't we believe in it? It is difficult to see the faults in the country in which we are born. But why should we care about our governments? Why should we care about other parts of the world that don't affect us? We're just people trying to live our lives.

"And who knows what's out there," I continued. "Who knows if it's any different from here?"

"Or any better."

But it must be. I yearned for it to be. If we're born into a nation that is unjust ... isn't it our duty to that very nation to rebel? Isn't it natural to want to know about the world around us, like I did as a child ... shouldn't we care about more than our selves, more than our families, more than our nations—but for *humanity*? There must be a world where the poor aren't abused and the authorities can't rape whoever they choose. At least it's what we ought to strive for.

How did speaking with Lauren always conjure up such thoughts of treason? I pushed them away. I had to solve this case. I had to find something to write about.

As if she had read my mind, Lauren's soft voice poked through the clouds:

"I know what you can do for writer's workshop."

"What?"

"Write my story."

Chapter Fifteen: The Idea

The doors to Huppington Books™ slowly opened as if being pulled apart by an invisible force, revealing the sky-blue eyes, the boxy head, and then the powerful figure of Vivek.

"I take you," he said. He turned and ambled past the automatrons and three-dimensional books with the violin case slung over his shoulder. I followed him into Huppington's office and watched as he lifted the painting behind Sylvester's desk as if it were as light as the bow of his violin.

"Vivek," he said, and the door materialized in the wall. We stepped through it and the cold air hit my face. The door vanished and it was completely dark. I took a step forward to start the descent down the spiral stairwell but my foot landed on Vivek's toes and I fell into his chest. He didn't budge.

I was with a man twice my size in absolute darkness! I didn't hold a chance against him without a weapon. Or would he throw me down the stairs?

"You want to know why I help you?" he asked.

"Yes, I do," I replied.

"You help beggars. I see you are a good man. But I am watching you."

There was a long, dark pause.

"Vivek want thanks."

"Oh," I said with a laugh. "Thank you, Vivek. You saved my ass."

"You're welcome,' he said, and stomped down the stairs. I followed the sound of his footsteps but couldn't help getting a bit dizzy, and when my foot searched for another step at the bottom of the stairwell, my balance lost, Vivek was there to stop me from falling.

The beam of light glided across Vivek's monstrous hand and the door opened with a buzz.

"Why does voice sound funny?" Vivek asked as we stepped out into the hallway.

"My voice? You're the one who sounds like one of those foreign bad guys you see in the movies—no offense."

"Your voice is higher than usual."

The voice modulator. It needed recharging.

"I'm ... sick," I explained, lowering my voice as much as I could. "Hey, can I ask you something? Why don't you live with Iryna? I mean, why do you live in the Slums if you don't have to?"

"Vivek like to be one with beggars. Vivek never forget where he came from. Like to play violin, fix cars, and ships. You? What are hobbies?"

"I like to watch blockball during the season, play cubes, see the occasional movie. But I don't have time for that kind of stuff. I have work."

"Career?"

"That's right."

"Career is all to many people. Sometimes, Vivek think, they forget to enjoy."

"Right, but whether we like it or not, our career often defines us in the eyes of other people. What's the first question you're asked by someone you're meeting for the first time? Is it not, 'what do you *do*?'"

"People busy with career and they forget big picture.

Try to enjoy life. This is what I do. This is what the old and wise say."

"We got to enjoy ourselves, sure, but we also have to earn a living. That's just the way of the world. The reality of life."

Vivek didn't respond. He ambled down the hall, silently. We walked past the rusty metal door of the weapons facility, its voice recognition box, and the vertical line of numbers, 0–9. I didn't care anymore about the case. The TPF officer had raped Lauren and The Chief did nothing to stop it. I had to write her story.

Or so I told myself at the time. There was still a side of me that clung to the past. Despite everything, I wasn't ready to give up on my childhood dream to become a detective nor was I able to forget my duty to The Nation. I know this now, as I write this, because I remember wondering if Vivek had access to the weapons facility; I remember trying to think of schemes to gain Sylvester's trust; I remember conjuring up images of the badge.

Vivek led me down the rest of the hallway in silence until we reached the door of writer's workshop. Its white paint was still peeling off.

"Go here."

"You don't say much, do you?"

"Less words, more do."

"I see."

I turned the old-fashioned knob and pushed open the door.

The workshop commenced. As I watched Sylvester lead it, I wondered how he had become the head of this group, how he had *created* it. How he had written an entire book about his life. After the last writer read their work, he concluded, "Now that writer's workshop is coming to an end, we will all introduce our writing plan for the next workshop. Let's start with Walter. What are you writing?"

You can't just write something. It has to come from the heart—but even that's not enough. You have to take that longing and put it into words—the best words possible so that what you want to say is clear, tangible, and at the same time, subtle, layered with meaning and truth. But to start is the hardest part. To *do* it. I know these things now, looking back to before I began writing this book. If I had known then what it was like to be a writer, I probably would not have said what I was about to say. The writers may have understood it if I had said, "I don't know how to start," if I had admitted my inadequacies. But if I had done that, you wouldn't be reading this right now.

"I have a friend. I said I'd write her story. Lauren worked for—" I stopped and looked at Sylvester. He was nodding his head. "She believed in something. And she was betrayed."

"We know your friend, Lauren," Sylvester remarked. "She vouched for you. Said you can be trusted. She is a talented poet and wrote nonfiction as well. Stopped attending writer's workshop all of a sudden. That sort of thing happens quite often here, with the risks involved. It's quite unfortunate."

Sylvester searched my eyes. Then he asked, "Do *you* feel betrayed, Walter?"

"I—" I felt lost for a moment, that unsettling feeling invading my being, that void expanding, and I could sense the others watching me. I breathed it away and finished, "need to write this book."

Sylvester's eyes widened. "A book?"

"Yes. Only a book will give justice to Lauren's story. I want it to sit on the shelves of the reading room, next to your autobiography, Sylvester, and all the other titles. I made a promise to my best friend."

The room got quiet. The writers eyed me curiously. Simon and Sara gazed in awe at me across the room. Sylvester was looking down at the table, a small smile forming on his lips.

It was then that I heard a large grunt. It was Sven, who had criticized Walter Cunningham's magazine. He examined me with those glassy-brown eyes, his droopy earlobes hanging by his cheeks, and asked, "So Walter, do you have a first chapter of this *book* to share? Every *writer*," he stressed, giving Sylvester a definitive glance before returning his gaze on me, "must share his writing with the rest of us."

"I've just come up with the idea. I haven't started it yet."

"How very ... *convenient*."

"And what the hell is that supposed to mean?"

"Enough." The room went silent at the sound of Sylvester's voice, not a shout, even and firm. Behind that voice was the forcefulness I detected when Sylvester commanded Iryna to put the gun away when I first met him in his office. It was a voice that commanded attention. "We must keep our solidarity. If Walter has just arrived at his idea, it is acceptable for him not to share today." Sven grunted through clenched teeth. "But you *must* share with us next time, Walter. Only those who share are invited into writer's workshop. See you all next time."

"Thank you, Sylvester," said Simon.

"Yah, thank you, Sylvestuh," Sara added. "For givin' us this place to write. To ex-press ourselves." The other writers all started thanking him as well, and I could see Sylvester's face changing to the expression I had seen when he toured me through ARM. It was of utter contentment, of a man who has made a difference in the lives of others.

"Thank you all for being here," Sylvester responded. "There would be no writer's workshop without writers!"

As I walked out of the writer's workshop room and into the hallway, my foot landed on something. I looked down to see that I had stepped on a wing of Ralph's butterfly. I lifted my foot and it tried to fly, taking off inches into the air and then falling back to the ground.

"Totally biznillidy!" Ralph exclaimed, strangely excited. He scooped it up with his hands. "I can touch it!" He turned to me. "What did you do?"

"I didn't mean to step on—"

"Oh no, I can fix her," he said, examining its delicate wing. "She'll fly again …" As he said this, he and the butterfly dissolved into the air.

I made my way through the limestone hallway, spotting Sylvester talking to Iryna a few feet away from the weapons facility. I walked past them to get to the exit when Sylvester took me by the arm.

"Hello, Walter. I think it's noble of you to write Lauren's story. Though I do wonder why you chose to write a *book*. Why not begin with something shorter? You could experiment with fiction by writing a short story."

"What's that?"

"Oh, dear. Hm. You're not ready to write this, are you? Don't respond to that." Sylvester looked around at the creators, who were making their way to the exit. "If you have time *now*, I could help you, one-on-one. We can return to the writer's workshop room—"

Here was a chance to get him one-on-one—to gain his trust. "Oh, great!" I exclaimed with much more enthusiasm than I had expected. The words came out without me even realizing it.

Sylvester was taken aback and gave me a confused look. "Actually, why don't you write independently first. Figure out what you want to write. Then come to me ... when you're *ready*."

Chapter Sixteen: The Turning Point

The City Courthouse was a large structure, with ten Doric columns lining the entrance, and above, inscribed from years past, were the words, "The True Administration of Justice is the Firmest Pillar of Good Government." At the top of the building was a silver statue of President Lapin. I leaned my head back and reread those words, looked at that statue, and wondered if justice would be done in Anji's case. It was finally the day of the verdict of *the Environmental Defense Group vs. Huppington Books*™.

When Tommy and I went inside the courthouse, the jurors were deciding, and we went to the balcony. I purposely came to the trial at the very end, wanting to spend as little time as I could and be as inconspicuous as possible. The last time I was in public with my son, Kenneth had manipulated a kid against him. I didn't want to take any chances.

I couldn't spot Kenneth anywhere in the courthouse, which was completely filled. It was a large room, as grand as The Mountain Theater, with portraits of famous judges lining its walls. From the balcony, I could just make out the large stomach of the judge, who sat on an elevated platform in the back of the spacious hall. I could have sworn I saw him munching on something. At the defendant's table, I spotted Anji, her hair neatly tied back. And even from where we were sitting, in the last row in the back, I could tell that the man sitting next to Anji was Sven, by his long, droopy earlobes.

Tommy tapped me on the shoulder, pointed behind us, and hid a laugh in his hand. There was a colossal portrait of the judge, looking fatter than ever.

A short old juror stood, mumbled "microphone" under her breath, and then spoke, in a booming amplified voice, which was much larger than she. "We, the jury, have decided in favor of Huppington Books™." A low murmur went through the crowd. Most of the people seemed displeased.

"Order!" the judge bellowed, his voice reaching far corners of the room as his double chins shook. "Thank you for your verdict, jurors. But I must overturn it. Paper books are adverse to the environment and are forms of resistance. Thus, I must rule in favor of the Environmental Defense Group. From this day forth, the publication of paper books is abolished." There was some clapping. Tommy looked around, confused. "In addition, books on UNICÉ or any form of the written word are from this day forth *prohibited*."

The courtroom went silent. "Government-mandated textbooks," the judge continued, "are permitted for educational purposes only. All information will be learned through Yabble© and UNITUBE. This case is dismissed."

Sven was out of his seat. "That's inequitable!" he yelled. "It's monstrous! I demand *justice!*" Anji put a hand on his shoulder.

"But that's not fair," Tommy said to me. "The jury decided one way and then the judge another."

"That's true, Tommy."

"And the judge outlawed all books … and the trial was about *paper* books."

"That's true too."

"It isn't fair. Mom lost and it just isn't fair."

I wanted to tell Tommy that you can't win every time. That law is a great profession and he shouldn't be discouraged by what he saw. That what The Nation decides is what's right for the people, even if it may not always seem that way. But as I watched the people leave the courtroom with faces of quiet apathy, and looked at my son, who was standing, gazing at the portrait of the judge, with a confused, embittered look on his face, I couldn't say anything at all.

The rays of the morning sun reflected off The Mountain. I couldn't find my pens, so I had to return to the antique shop. I stepped onto the skytrain, and found a spot by the window, where I could view The Mountain's triangular shadow against The City skyline. As the train swooped through the clouds, The Mountain came closer, and a young boy jumped up and down, pulling on his mother's shirt. "It's the biggest thing I've ever seen!" he cried out, pointing at it. I turned away from his gummy smile, and looked at the carbon tubes that connected to form the tower's exterior as we came into the portal. I wondered what would happen if I twisted one of those tubes until it came off. When I looked at the tiny silver tubing that held it all together, The Mountain didn't seem so big after all.

I got stuck behind a group of college boys on the mechanized walkway. One of the boys was bragging about how he slept with a girl the night before whom he met at a club in the Entertainment District. "She was super hot," he kept saying but the boys pretended not to believe him. "She had huge tits." The kid cupped his hands in front of his chest. "Double D's. I snuck a peek at her bra." When he said that, I had a strange urge to sock him in the face. No one wanted to hear how he convinced some girl to sleep with him because she had "huge tits."

I forced myself into the elevator, pushing people so I could get in front of the voice panel and say, "234." A tall man stepped on my foot as he squeezed by me. He mumbled an indifferent, "Sorry."

"It's fine," I said, glancing at him.

Then I looked again. He had distinguished gray hair, sharp brown eyes, and was tall and thin. I studied his profile, that face—he seemed really familiar.

The man got off at my floor and walked in the very direction I was going. I stood behind him on the mechanized walkway. Then, as we approached the antique shop, he got off the walkway and went inside.

I followed him through the aging forest scent to the back of the room, where the old man was sitting on his wooden stool. The man stuck his hand into his pocket, shuffled around, and then pulled something out with his fingers. He plopped it on the counter. It was gold, had an engraving of an eagle, and silver letters that read 'DETECTIVE.' I recognized that badge.

"Holy shit!" I found myself saying. I looked up at the man. "You're Detective Conrad! The greatest detective The City has ever seen."

"So I am," he replied in a gruff voice.

"I'm also a detective. Victor. Victor Vale."

"Nice to meet you."

"Actually, we met before. I was just a child, I'm sure you don't remember—"

The old man cleared his throat. "Selling?"

"Yes," Detective Conrad said, glancing at me through the corner of his eye. "How much can I get for it?"

"But that's your *badge*! Why would you sell that??"

"Listen," he said. "I need the money. Now stop bothering me."

"That badge—it's given you such respect. You can't sell that. You owe it to the force. To the people."

"Listen, kid," he said. I couldn't remember the last time someone called me "kid." "I don't owe anybody anything. You know what the force did for me? Gave me a lifetime of bad memories and a pension plan that barely provided me with enough cash to go on a vacation. And the people? What did they ever do for *me*?"

I just stood there, speechless, watching Detective Conrad sell his badge to the crotchety old man. If this was how Detective Conrad ended up ... what would become of me? My dream, to get a detective badge, what I had longed for since I was a child, it all meant nothing. It all came crashing down in that moment. I felt faint, the room became blurry, and I nearly fell to the floor. But then my eyes met the notepads stacked in a pile in the front of the shop. I knew what I had to do.

But when I returned to my office, I couldn't write. I didn't know how. I thought when I put the pen to the page words would come out—but no. This was work. I even put on my disguise, thinking that if I became Walter Cunningham, inspiration would magically surge to my brain and through my fingers. But I didn't know where to start. Where does a man begin writing another man's story (or in this case, a woman)? The day I met her at the Academy? The day she was born? I didn't know her as a child. I didn't know her past. I didn't know her thoughts or feelings. This wasn't my story. It was Lauren's.

I opened my nanokit and stuck a needle into my arm.

"Lauren? Are you there? Walter Cunningham needs

his muse."

No answer.

Lauren was always on UNICÉ. I went to the cubes room. The seats were empty. The cubes hovered over the board, waiting to be played. I reached my hand out toward one of the pieces and it flew to the top of the ceiling. The rest of the cubes shot out in different directions and I stumbled backwards to the floor. The ceiling began to crumble and fall and then—whoosh— it changed to a setting sky. I pushed myself up and found myself standing on the road. Ahead was the purple sun. It was strange; I didn't mean to *transform*. I walked. Watched people's faces as I passed them by. They scowled at me. A kid spat in my face. They called me selfish, they called me a traitor, they said, "How could you return that badge?" "That's not me!" I shouted. That's not me. I came to the end of the road. The sun was bright. I shielded my eyes. I looked away. Then the sun had changed. It had an entrance. Two purple doors. I wanted to go inside. But a man stood in front. It was the judge. He blocked the doors with his enormous body. Then he laughed. And laughed.

"Return!" I shouted. "Return!"

I was at my desk, feeling as if I had awakened mid-dream. I took a deep breath. I didn't mean for that to happen. I wasn't like Ralph from ARM and the other druggies. Only those addicted to UNICÉ *transformed* enough so that the virtual world broke into reality. That hadn't happened yet, but this was weird, because it was out of my control.

Where was Lauren?

My mind hazy, I wanted to stay out of virtual world for a while; I didn't even want to transmit into a hologram. So I took the skytrain to Lauren's apartment, still in disguise as Walter Cunningham.

The door to her apartment was unlocked so I let myself inside. It was a wreck. There was a pile of dirty dishes in the sink, underwear on the floor, tissues scattered everywhere. A light was left on in the kitchen and it smelt like spoiled food. "Lauren? Did you hear about the trial?" I walked into the hallway. "I need to talk to you about this book. I don't know how to start it. I think you should write it. Or at least we could do it together. Lauren?" I came to the living room. "Where are y—?"

I can't begin to describe what I saw next. It hurts too much. But for Lauren, I have to try. She was sitting on the couch, naked, a needle hanging out of her vein. Her head was tilted back, and her eyes were open and vacant. Her wrists, they were … bleeding. And where the needle hung, in the crook of her elbow, there was blood oozing out.

I was shaking her. "Lauren? Get off UNICÉ! What have you done??" I was in a dream, I told myself. This wasn't happening.

I slowly removed the needle from her arm, hardly able to watch, biting down on my lip so hard it bled. I wrapped a cloth around her to stop the bleeding, called for an ambulance, and then picked her up and carried her into the hallway, her head bobbing up and down, in and out of the elevator, and finally to the exit of her building. The ambulance had just arrived and it was there that I knew it had happened, when the EMTs stopped trying. I screamed, without even realizing it, a cry of anguish, in the form of an incomprehensible growl. Those aqua eyes had become a vacant stare, her lips purple and cold, her body white. She was always good, desperately trying to connect to something real, and cared for others—for me. As I looked at once was, a word escaped my lips:

Lapin.

I waited at the hospital until the doctor said it. And then I ran. I ran out of the hospital and shoved my way through the head scanner and onto the skytrain. After it swung into the center of the Round Tower, I bolted out through the skytrain doors, down the mechanized walkway, until out of breath, I was standing in front of Huppington Books. I put my mouth to the recognition box.

"Walter Cunningham here."

"Image or real?"

"Real."

"Walter?" It was Iryna's voice. "ARM won't meet for at least a week because of the trial. Until things settle down."

"I'm here to see Sylvester."

"Oh. Hold on."

The large purple doors opened. Sylvester was standing there.

"I'm ready," I said. "I'm ready to begin my story."

Part III

The Book

Chapter Seventeen: How It Began

It was only Sylvester and I in the writer's workshop room. He motioned to the seat beside him. As I sat, I could hear the legs of the chair grinding against the floor. Every movement I made—putting my pad to the table, pressing the top of my pen so it clicked, my breath—sounded louder than usual. Sylvester put on his round spectacles and adjusted his watch. He opened the pad, empty except for the poem I had written with Lauren.

"I want to write a book about the world we live in. About the corruption of the TPF. And the lies of President Lapin."

"Hold on!" Sylvester exclaimed, putting up his hand. "Let's start small." His tone was business-like and his look serious."The grand ideas will come out naturally with fine-tuned prose and characterization. We'll start with some writing exercises. I want you to write about things you care about. What matters to you. Take a minute to write. And no talking. With your whole life speaking on UNICÉ, you need to get used to the written word." He leaned his arm across mine and wrote, in a compellingly illegible scrawl:

What matters?

I wrote:

Money

He scribbled:

What else?

I wrote:

$
$$
$$$
$$$$
$$$$$$
$$$$$$$$$$$$$$$

I looked up. He wrote:

Really?

Yes. Stability. Security. We have to earn money for our families.

There must be more.

But $ is practical, it's how we get by I know $ I have $ raised a son who is accustomed to $ my wife values $

Money has only the value we give it.

But we give it all the value in the world. So it matters. Look at the beggars.

What else do you care about?

My family. My wife and son.

Good. Let's start at the beginning. How about your parents?

I was adopted.

Have you ever sought out your birth parents?

Yes. But I have no desire to see them anymore.

Why not?

Why should I? They abandoned me.

I want you to write about your family. To reach into your past. Was there anything you wrote, maybe something from your childhood?

I don't think so.

Why not search on UNICE?

    I went through images on the lens of my glasses like they were slides, shifting from one to the next. Then I saw it.

You found something?

Yes. A story I wrote when I was eight years old.

Write one paragraph explaining the story to someone who doesn't know anything about it. To your reader.

But it's written by a child.

That's all right. Transcribe it in its truest form.

I put down my pen. "Look, Sylvester …"

"I said no talking."

"I know, but I have to say, I know you're supposed to share your writing … but I feel restricted with you looking over my shoulder, and I feel like it's inhibiting my ability to write. Would it be all right if I shared with you a section—say this story I wrote here—but wait to share the rest?" It was true—I did feel restricted with Sylvester there. Besides, if I wanted to write honestly, I couldn't have Sylvester reading this, or he'd know right away that I was a detective.

Sylvester hummed in disapproval. But he acquiesced. "All right, Walter, I don't want you to feel censored. Just don't tell the other writers. Now get writing."

I picked up my pen. And began to write:

My third grade teacher used to read us the Bible. She told us never to eat from the tree of knowledge or God would punish us like Adam and Eve. I found myself writing as she lectured. It was then that I wrote my first story:

My Genesis

What if insted of banishing Adam and Eve God gave them a choclat chip cookie. When they ate the cookie they became giants and ruled all the animals. But they were good to the animals and they kept them as pets. If any of the animals were meen, the snake, who was a giant too from eating Eves cookie crums wood swallow the animal hole. Then one day God got jelus of the snake and he killed him with a thunder. Adam and Eve got mad at God and they killed HIM. Then Adam and Eve ruled as King and Queen of the hole world and they had Cain and Abel, who had children, who had more children and so humans were made.

Sylvester wrote:

A child may have limited experience but he can tell the difference between right and wrong. So you have written creatively before. Keep writing. How did you feel about the story after you wrote it? And what happened when your teacher saw the story? Your parents? Tell me about your childhood. Write at least five full paragraphs.

"Sure. But don't look, please."

"All right, Walter," he said with a sigh. "I'll go into a corner of the room and write myself. Call me over if you need me."

I wrote:

It was nonsense of course. But more than the story itself, I enjoyed the *making* of it. At the supermarket, I asked my mother to buy one of every kind of apple they had. When I got home, I took a bite out of each one. I had expected some sort of magical surge of knowledge to zip through my arms and reach my head, but no—I just tasted an apple's sweetness that was never so disappointing. When my mother saw six apples with six little teeth marks, I told her I wanted to taste knowledge like Eve had. She called my teacher, and I had "a talk" with her and my adoptive parents. My father said that everything I needed to know came from home and school and UNICÉ. If I wanted to stay in Eden, I shouldn't question God.

My adoptive father was a businessman. Not once did he speak of my real father. When I was thirteen, my mother told me I was adopted. I told her I didn't care about my biological parents. Why should I? They didn't give a shit about me. I wouldn't talk about them. My adoptive father had taken me in for his wife, who couldn't have a child after she had George, and he never thought of me as a real son. He was obsessed with his work; he didn't have time for me. Then what happened to his son—I took the blame. All I wanted to do was escape from my father and that house. I kept seeing visions of George in our room: resting in bed, the top bunk, or reaching into the closet for an illegal brush.

I wanted to become a detective. But my mother insisted I go to college first. My father paid for it—he was more than happy to get rid of me. On the day I left home, my mother told him to give me some "fatherly advice." Grudgingly, he took me aside, and said, "It's a rough world but a good one; have faith in God, in The Nation, but most of all, in yourself. Provide for yourself and your family. No one else will." I told myself I didn't care about anything he said. But I still remember those words to this day.

He didn't reply to my messages when I started my studies. So I stopped messaging him. I heard that my mother died shortly after I left home. I went home for the funeral and everyone acted nice to me for a while after. I rarely talked about her though. I couldn't bear to think about it.

And then a strange thing started to happen. I began to feel a void, an emptiness, as if a part of me was missing. I found myself catching my reflection in mirrors, on computer screens, in bottles of beer, wondering where my eyes came from, my hair. I started to seek out my real parents, scanning UNICÉ for people who looked like me. Even more, I wanted to know if I had a brother or sister.

Around that time, I met Anji and everything changed. She got pregnant. I stopped investigating the past and started looking toward the future. I needed to make money. I had to prove to Anji that I wasn't marrying her because of who her father was. There were openings at the police force, and before I knew it, I was wearing a blue uniform and carrying a gun. I started working the day after I graduated from college and never looked back. I was ambitious. I knew I had the skills to become a detective. I wanted that badge.

Then Tommy was born. I got the promotions I wanted. My son was smart and ambitious and listened to his parents … sometimes. He wanted to be a lawyer like his mother and his grandfather. He wanted to play blockball like his father.

I accepted the world for what it was and it accepted me.

"Finished."

Sylvester ambled toward me and jotted on my pad with his silver pen:

How do you feel?

Surprised. That I wrote that. It was difficult to find the right words. But now I feel good.

Writing isn't easy. In fact, writing my first book was one of the hardest things I have ever done. But there's something special writers feel when our words form on the page. Here's what you're going to do next. You've told us about your childhood. Now I'd like you to show it. With descriptions, characters, and dialogue. A complete scene. Write about a significant incident in your past.

The first significant event in my life that I can remember happened when I was ten. I was with my mother in the kitchen, playing with my Mini-Automatron as I slurped a bowl of cereal. The Mini-A was in the shape of a boy with the mind of a computer and it was the size of an outstretched hand. I flipped open the phone by unfolding the boy's 'head', 'arms', and 'legs'. I liked to talk through the holes in his 'cheeks' and listen through his 'mouth', but I was most mesmerized by his eyes. The eyebrows lifted in satisfaction or disapproval but his eyes didn't move. Yet on occasion, at certain times I couldn't predict, I caught myself looking into those eyes, and discerning some sort of indefinable expression.

My mother was baking an apple pie and its scent slowly crept out of the oven. Apple pie was my brother's favorite dessert.

There were three loud raps at the door. I watched from behind the bowl of cereal as my mother took out the pie and lumbered out of the kitchen. I wondered if I had enough time to take a quick bite of the pie without her seeing and imagined what they would do to me if they found out I did.

A holographic image of a man in an oversized nanojacket and a gentle smile across his face stood outside the door. When he saw my mother, he reached inside his jacket pocket, and pulled out a badge. "I'm Detective Conrad," he said.

When my mother saw the detective's badge, she greeted him with a wide, welcoming smile.

"Oh, do come in, detective. Everything is all right, isn't it?"

"I'm afraid not."

He spotted my eyes, peering over the rim of the cereal bowl. "Hello there," he said. I was too timid to respond.

"What's the matter, Detective?"

The detective whispered, "The TPF are coming. They got a tip that there are creators here. They will be raiding this area any minute."

I could hear the creaking of my father's office door opening from the second floor. Then came his rough, aggravated voice, clear enough that it could carry down the stairs, without him having to shout, "Who let this man inside?"

The detective took a moment to respond. "Heed my warning—"

"I heard you. There is no need for that, here. Nobody in this house has engaged in illegal activities of any kind. I have to get back to work. So if you wouldn't mind, get out of my house!" The door slammed shut behind him.

"I'll take my leave," Detective Conrad said. He looked over at me, gave a slight wave of the hand, and disintegrated into the air. My mother walked over to the pie, and with her back turned, I bolted up the stairs and charged into my bedroom.

"The TPF are coming!" I shouted.

"What are you talking about?" George asked. George was tall, six years older than me, always told me what to do, and never listened to a word I said. But he was the only one who gave a shit about me.

"A detective just told Mom!"

"Are you sure you heard him right? Or was it your imagination running wild again?"

I still remember the sound I heard next. It was the whirring of a TPF helicopter. George and I locked eyes. It was the first time either of us had heard it. But everyone knew what it meant.

George reached into the closet. He pulled out a laser driver.

"I need your help," he said. "You can fit under the bed. Crawl under it and laser through the floorboards. I'll hide my stuff in there."

"No!"

"What do you mean, *no!*"

"I don't want to get in trouble!"

"Do you *hear* the helicopter? Do you *know* what the officers would do to me if they found out??"

I could hear the pounding of boots outside the open window.

"Fine!" I said with a loud grunt. I crawled under the bed. It was dark, and I was surrounded by clumps of dirt and two different colored socks. George handed me the laser driver and I undid the nails from two long blocks of wood. I put them to the side and placed my hands into the empty space where they had been. It was black; I couldn't see what was in there.

"Here," he said, handing me an easel. "Don't touch the canvas, it's still drying."

"Ugh!" I held it by its cool wooden frame and finagled it into the space as gingerly as I could. Even in that moment of danger, I felt an impetuous desire to see what George was risking his life for.

"Hey, Sylvester!" He was hunched in a corner, deep in writing. My voice ripped through the incredible silence that permeated the writer's workshop room. "I just wrote the word 'impetuous.' That's a good one, isn't it?"

He walked over to me and scribbled:

Write, Walter.

Did I spell it correctly?

Yes. Write.

As I put the easel inside, I squinted my eyes to make out the painting in the dark. Though I couldn't be sure, I thought I could see the outline of a butterfly.

"Why the heck are you painting butterflies? Are you a *girl*?"

"Ha ha," George said sarcastically.

"Seriously though, why?"

"Promise you won't laugh."

"Okay, fine."

"To me, no matter how ugly the world gets, butterflies will always be beautiful."

"Wow. You *are* a girl."

"Shut up. Here." George handed me a large metal jar. "And here." He pushed another under the bed.

"OMG!" I shouted. "How many do you have?"

The front door of the house swung open so loudly that I could hear it slamming against the wall.

"They're here! Take it!" George gave me a handful of paintbrushes. I dropped them inside. "Cover it up! Hurry!"

I lasered the pieces of wood back into place and came out from under the bed. We looked at each other—the "we did it" look. My mother was calling for us to come downstairs.

"Yes, mom!" he replied as casually as he could, walking out of the bedroom.

I noticed one of George's brushes sticking out of the door of his closet. It was dripping fresh red paint. I wanted to tell George but he was already at the top of the stairs, and the floorboards were already sealed, so I took it, and not knowing what else to do, I stuck it down my pants. I looked down at my shirt. It was covered with streaks of red.

"I need to see every member of the household." I could hear the TPF officer talking to my father. "You have only one child?"

"Yes …" My father paused. In that moment, I felt like I was being eaten up inside. "And then there's Victor."

My parents wouldn't protect me. I had to escape. I got onto the dresser and looked out the window. There was the elm tree, with its thickest branch just a few feet from the windowsill. I had imagined myself leaping onto that tree and climbing down. I even dreamt about it: about escaping, going off on my own, and discovering the world. I thought it was just a dream. But there I was, staring at the elm tree's rough, fat limb, jutting out toward the window. Judging its distance, I saw new possibilities, and my dreams took shape into an artificial reality of mountains and oceans, and I thought to myself, that all I had to do was jump—

I was in the air. My little fingers tried to grasp the branch, but then I could feel it slipping away, and I fell—

Into a man's arms. It was Detective Conrad. He's here to get me, too, I thought, and I tried to run.

"Hold on a second!" he shouted. "Are you all right?"

I struggled to break free from him but his grip was too strong.

"I'm trying to help—" he said, and he took his hand and reached into my pants. I squealed as he pulled out the brush. "If I let go of you, will you trust me?"

"No!" I said. "You're going to *arrest* me!"

He took me by my wrists and forcibly turned me around so I faced him.

"A detective's job is to protect the people. We don't just *arrest* them for no reason." He let go of one of my wrists and put the brush into his jacket pocket. I watched as red paint fell from the brush onto the front of his jacket. I stopped trying to run, and he let go of me.

He took his detective badge out of his pocket. I had never seen anything like it. It looked like pure gold. I was mesmerized by the engraving of the eagle and the silver letters … DETECTIVE. It was covered in what I thought was blood. The detective took out a piece of cloth and wiped off the red paint, which was sliding down the eagle's feathers and into the grass. It was the coolest thing I had ever seen.

"Sorry about your badge," I said.

He gave me a funny look. "I thought you were bleeding, kid. Turn your shirt around. You know, your neighbor over there—" he pointed across the street. "And over there—" he pointed in the opposite direction. "They would have been caught by the TPF if I hadn't been around. I'm telling you, you gotta stop doing what you're doing, because there aren't many people like me left. And you're just a kid. If you creators don't stop, they're gonna find you, and soon, all of you, are gonna be gone—"

A loud bang came from inside the house. It was the first gunshot I ever heard. The noise sailed into my eardrums and to the crevices of my brain. From that day on, in the shadows of the night, and under the rays of the sun, I can still hear a faint murmur in my ears.

How do you feel?

Whoa. That was incredibly painful. To relive the moment of my brother's death. But I guess I feel

179

accomplished too. And a sense of … relief.

Those are natural feelings. You've started your book.

Look away, please. I want to address the reader.

I think I wrote that story because I needed to find why I wanted to become a detective in the first place. Maybe now I can move past it.

"What should I write next?" I asked, cutting into the silence.

"It's past midnight," Sylvester said. "Let's continue this tomorrow."

"No. I want to keep going."

"Are you sure?" he asked.

I nodded my head. I wanted that silence back, where the only sound was the soft scribbling of the pen on the page. I relished the feeling of my entire being becoming devoted to one and only one thing, and where all distractions, plans for the future, and anxieties of the past, were forgotten, and I could just be in the moment and write. The void I had been feeling … had miraculously lifted.

"All right, then," he said. "Let's move forward in time."

He scribbled:

Write about the first time you started to get these feelings … about the world we live in. When a change in your thoughts or your beliefs began.

"What if I get stuck?"

Tap into your subconscious mind. If you get stuck, don't try to fight it. If you're really struggling, close your eyes and clear your mind. The ideas will come. Now write. Where does your story begin?

Hm. Well, when was it when I first felt like something was missing? I've always felt it to some extent because of the absence of my parents. But more recently … it was the day that I walked through the Slums and Kenneth shot that beggar. And maybe I was affected by it because the beggar's *brother* witnessed the murder … just as I had heard the gunshot that killed George. Yes, that's it. That's where my story begins.

So I write:

Not long after the Cleansing Act, I was promoted to Detective.

Chapter Eighteen: The Gift

I watched the rays of the sun eke out from the sides of The Mountain as I rode the skytrain home. While the people around me were darting their pupils back and forth, lost on UNICÉ, I couldn't stop thinking about the words I had put on the page. I would not go on UNICÉ; I didn't *need* to. I had begun to write my book.

The Mountain looked like a dark pyramid against the orange and yellow aura of the setting sun. I thought about how it was at The Mountain where I bought this pad, its cool wooden cover pressing against my chest, hidden beneath the layers of my nanojacket. It felt right having the pad so close; one cannot predict when or how ideas will come. Then my mind wandered to the first words I wrote, and I was struck with thoughts of George—the memory that I had uncovered. I hadn't given much thought to the danger I was putting myself in when Sylvester used nanoglue to attach the pad securely to my undershirt. The other passengers seemed to be looking at me one second but not the next. I had to get somewhere safe. I'd be having dinner with Anji and Tommy in an hour. There had to be somewhere I could put my pad away from my wife and son, but near enough to me in case inspiration hit. Although it was George who was killed that day, it could have been me—George had risked *my* life by creating. He had risked the lives of his family.

The TPF still raided creators every day. I had gotten rid of that terrible feeling of something missing in my life, I believed—I had found it in writing. But at what cost?

When I arrived at the apartment, I entered the bedroom with my pad, and told the door to "lock". I took a laserdriver out of the toolkit in my closet and shot at four nails on a piece of wood in the floorboards under the bed. I undid the nails and lifted up the piece of wood. I placed the pad in there. For a split second, I thought I saw George's face on the cover of the pad.

I put the piece of wood back, shooting the laser at the nails so they screwed back into place. As I put the laserdriver back in the toolkit, I looked at the wooden blockball bat, leaning against the closet wall. The way I felt when I connected with the ball in my high school days, it was just how I felt yesterday, when my pen released its ink onto the page.

Free

There was a knock at the door. Anji was in her office, Tommy in his room—who was here? I walked into the hallway. A second knock—I went into my office, to the closet, and took out my liquidator. Heard the sound of someone fumbling with the doorknob. Came back into the hallway and pointed the liquidator at the door, the knob turning slowly in front of me. As I came closer and closer to the door, imaging the TPF on the other side, my finger shook as it rested on the trigger, and then the door opened with a click.

He held out his hand and took a step back. "Do not shoot!" It was Henry, with shopping bags in his hands, which he dropped to the ground.

"Sorry, Henry."

"Henry will prepare dinner now," he said, picking

up the bags, taking three steps into the apartment, pivoting on both heels, turning, and marching into the kitchen. I took a deep breath. I went back into my office and opened the closet door. As I placed the liquidator back in the closet, my hand was shaking.

A high-pitched giggle came from Tommy's room. I tiptoed down the hall and leaned my ear to the door. Sure enough, there was a girl in there.

"Open."

As the door opened, Tommy slid across the floor, pushing a book under his bed. And there was Amber, sitting on the floor with her legs crossed, two purple pigtails draped against her shoulders. I noticed a fresh bruise imbedded in her freckles.

Tommy put his hands behind his back.

"Give me whatever you have in your hands," I ordered. He took his right hand out from behind his back. He was holding a stack of pens and a white marker.

"Those are *my* pens! Did you go into my *office*?"

Amber was watching me with a look of fear across her face. I reached under the bed and pulled out the book, my hand still shaking. It was a notepad, the same kind he had before.

"Dad, I'm really so—"

I put up a finger. "Sh." I opened the book. There were drawings of Amber, Ms. Hiccup, blockball, videotron characters. I closed the book and handed it back to Tommy.

"There are some good pictures here."

Amber gave a large, toothy smile.

"You mean you're not mad at me?" Tommy asked.

"I don't want you drawing *anywhere*," I said. Amber stopped smiling and Tommy took a sigh of disappointment. "Except in your room. Is that

185

understood? Find a better hiding place. And for God's sake, lock your door."

"Okay, Dad," Tommy replied, smiling.

"Let me see that white marker for a second."

"This?" Amber asked, taking it out of Tommy's hand and holding it in front of me.

"I'll have that," I said, snatching it out of Amber's hand. She frowned. "Tommy can keep the pens though. Are you joining us for dinner?"

"I'm eating with my dad tonight," squeaked Amber. "He wants to meet you, Tommy. I've told him all about you."

I noticed then that Tommy's blond bangs had been cut. "Hey, what happened to your hair?"

"I cut it," Amber responded. "They were getting in the way of his eyes. He couldn't even see his own drawings."

Tommy's blond bangs. Me, Anji, her parents, we all had dark hair. It must have come from one of my parents.

I looked at her and then at Tommy. "Are you two …?"

"DAD! Leave us alone!"

"I have to go home, anyway." Amber stood up, puckered her lips, and blew a kiss to Tommy. "I always wanted to do that!" she said with a giggle and her image faded into the air.

"There's my boy!" I exclaimed.

"Her dad said that she could date boys now. And then she asked me out."

"Wow. I couldn't even talk to girls at your age …"

"Hey, Dad … what's a French kiss? Some of the boys were talking about it. Charlie said he already did it twice. But is it really when you touch a girl's tongue? It sounds gross."

I couldn't help but laugh. "Yes, that's what it is. I know it seems gross but actually, it's kind of nice. If it feels right, and Amber wants to, then kiss her."

"How will I know when it feels right?"

"You'll just know. And when you do, don't let fear get in the way. That's what stopped me from kissing a girl for a long time. Now let's have dinner."

Now that exams were over, Tommy was finally having dinner with us again and Henry was cooking steak—which took exactly three minutes to zap well done. When Henry left to the recharge room, I double-checked the front door to see that it was locked even though I had heard it click. I thought I was being paranoid but I also knew that the door could be forced open with the strength of a TPF officer's arm, and the lock could be picked by the adroitness of a steady hand.

I hadn't eaten all day and I devoured my meal. Tommy was strangely quiet though. When Tommy was quiet, he had something eating at him, something he had to get off his chest or else he'd sit alone in his room and speak to nobody but himself.

"Soo, how were your exams?" Anji asked.

"I think I did good."

"Well," I corrected. "It's, 'I think I did well.' It's a very common mistake."

"When did you become concerned with grammar all of a sudden?" Anji asked incredulously.

"Just preparing our son for his exams."

We kept munching on our steaks. As I went for a bite, I felt tension in the air. It was coming from my son.

"Mom," Tommy said. "I'm really sorry about the trial."

"That's sweet of you to say, Tommy." Anji responded. "I'm sorry too. But there will be more trials. I did my best and that's all I can do."

"You hear that, Tommy? That's a very mature way of looking at it," I said. Anji never ceased to surprise me. That trial was everything to her—I feared she would be crushed by it if she lost. Yet she was handling it shockingly well. I think she knew that the odds were stacked against her—that she would probably lose. She had accepted it somewhere along the line. But what Tommy was about to say—that was something she wasn't ready for.

"Mom. I have to tell you something."

Anji looked at me, asking with her eyes if I knew what he was talking about, and I shook my pupils "no."

"I don't want to be a lawyer anymore."

Anji's fork fell from between her fingers and landed on her plate with a loud clank.

"Don't be silly, that's what you've always wanted," she said.

"That's what *you've* always wanted!" he shouted. He looked down at his food and quietly added, "Amber said that I should be honest with you about it."

Anji looked at me to help her. I pretended that I couldn't speak because of a mouthful of meat.

"What do you want to do then?" she asked.

"Portraits?" he spoke more as a question than as an answer.

"Portraits? You can't make a decent living from portraits. Don't you want to make money? Provide for your family? These things are important, Tommy. Painting, well, you need to have a *gift* for it. One in a million actually do. You have to be practical in life."

I thought back to the manuscript hidden under the floorboards of our bed. What if Anji found it in her quest to stabilize her Qi?

Well, this is *my* Qi, Anji. The pages I'm writing now.

Even if you don't believe I have it in me.

"Dad?" Tommy turned to me. "Do I draw good?"

"You knew about this?"

"He just told me."

"Well, then tell him. Tell your son what it is we want him to do with his future."

I looked at my wife, I looked at my son, and I realized that I had received my wish—we were talking, like families used to do before UNICÉ wove its way into our brains. Our first family dinner in weeks, and there I was, forced to take the side of my wife or my son.

When I looked into Tommy's eyes, I saw myself. Do I write well? Do I need to have the gift to do something that makes me feel happy?

"I think Tommy should do what he wants with his life," I finally said. There was a short silence.

"So I'm the bad guy?" Anji asked. Her eyes were beginning to swell with tears.

"No, mom!" Tommy said. "I just … well, I guess I thought about doing portraits of famous people. I don't know why, I just like to do it. And Dad says they're good."

"They are good, Tommy, but do think about what Mom said. You don't need to make this decision right now."

"I know, Dad. That's the thing. I mean, I *think* I want to be a portraitist. But really … I don't know what I want. That's the truth, Mom."

"Who's going to take over the firm?" Anji sputtered, her little nose reddening. "Dad started it for us …" Anji took a deep breath. When she tried to breathe again it was a struggle. Her breath shortened and she gave a loud, high-pitched wheeze. "Get her jacket!" I screamed at Tommy, whose eyes were suddenly alert and he ran out of the room and came back in a flash with the salbutamol jacket. He wrapped it around her with a hug as she continued to wheeze. "I'm sorry, Mom!" he cried.

As the jacket released its menthol particles, Anji's panting became slower and deeper until she was able to breathe normally again. She put her arms around Tommy's back, holding him tightly as she began to cry. Anji so rarely cried. Tommy let her tears wet his new shirt. I put my hand on Anji's shoulder. She brushed it away.

Chapter Nineteen: Sylvester's Proposition

ARM continued a week later. The TPF stormed into Huppington Books™ … wait. I don't have to write "™"! The TPF stormed into Huppington Books and erased all the data off the main computer. They went to the back of the Round Tower by the line of apple trees and discovered the paper book archive, where they sprayed the books with their green, snake-like hoses. The creators found the books soaking in stoplight red buckets. When they carefully lifted them out of the warm water, the pages stuck together, pieces falling through their fingers to the floor. Sylvester tried to dry them. But all he could see was an illegible mess, letters fused together like discordant ideas.

Lapin announced that no book would ever be published again. All paper books were to be "watered", which the newsman defined as "sprayed and soaked until rendered unreadable". They were placed in sinks and bathtubs throughout The Nation. Homes were raided, citizens arrested. Anyone involved in the publication of a book was to be punished with life imprisonment.

During that week, I wrote 191 pages of this manuscript.

Vivek patted down the creators as they entered ARM. He did it in the hallway so everyone could see. The Chief had told me that there was a TPF officer undercover in ARM, and I still didn't know who he or she was.

Writer's workshop began again, and those with courage returned. The writers were more somber than before, but none of them had lost their desire to write. I sat in the chair next to Sylvester, where I had written most of this manuscript, and where Sven usually sat. When Sven entered the room, he glared suspiciously in my direction, and then took a seat across the table.

Sylvester took out an old-fashioned, brown leather briefcase. It had three gold dials with the numbers one through nine, indicating a secret code, but all you needed to do to open the thing was to pull two golden tabs on the end of the briefcase to the side. He slid it across the table to me, Sven shifted his eyes from Sylvester to the briefcase to me. I put my manuscript inside.

"Ooh, is that for your book?" Sara asked, trotting over to me from the door.

"Yes, Sara."

"Wow. How far 'long *are* you?" she asked in a small voice. She leaned over the table with one hand pressing against it, lifting her foot slightly off the ground when she spoke.

"Oh, I don't know, maybe … 191 pages."

"Wow!" she said, touching my arm. "How long's it gonna be?"

"I don't know. As long as it needs to be, I guess."

Simon came into the room with a baby. Its face was covered with patches of dirt and its clothes were torn.

"'Ave you met my son?" Sara asked me.

"What is a kid doing here?"

"Whaddya mean?" she asked, crumpling up her brow.

"You shouldn't have brought him here. Does your

husband have any sense? This is a place with illegal activities. The TPF could come at any moment. Your son could get killed."

"Now hold on a second," Simon said, approaching me. "This is our *son*. It's not any of your business—"

"This is no place for children!" I shouted. Everyone was looking at me. Even Sylvester shot me a look. The baby started to cry.

"He's right," said Simon. "I'll come back tomorrow." He studied me for a moment and then left with the sobbing baby. Sara sat at the other side of the table, trying to avoid the stares of the other writers.

"I'm sorry," I said to the room. "This just isn't a place for children, that's all." With her chin resting in her hand, Sara gazed at me, lost in thought.

"Shall we begin then?" Sylvester asked, scratching his head. "Who would like to read their work?"

"How about Walter?"Sven asked, giving me a sly smile. "I know you've written something. It's in the briefcase Sylvester gave you."

"I have … but it's not where it needs to be yet."

"Of course it isn't," Sven scoffed. "If you actually wrote 191 pages in a single week, it is doubtful they would be any good."

"Now, Sven," Sylvester said. "We're here to support each other. I don't think that criticism was necessary."

"I don't mean to be opprobrious," he said to Sylvester. "I'm just curious."

"What?" I asked.

"Opprobrious, Walter, or do you not know what that word means? Abusive, hateful, exhibiting unkind behavior or words."

"We don't all mem-rize the dictionary, like you, Sven," Sara remarked.

He ignored her and looked at me. "What genre would

you say your book is?"

"Genre?"

"Yes, *genre*: fiction, nonfiction, creative nonfiction …"

"Nonfiction. Well, actually, maybe creative nonfiction."

"Do you even know the distinction between the two?"

"I think I can figure it out."

"This isn't a cross-examination—" Sylvester began to say.

"What is your book *about*, Walter?"

"My book," I paused, looking Sven straight in the eye, "is about *you*."

"Me?"

I looked into the eyes of the other writers. "It's about ARM. I want to expose the lies that have been fed to us by The Nation. It's not just about what happened to Lauren—it's about the world we live in. How technology is getting out of hand. I want to show a side of our system that is often overlooked."

The room went quiet.

Sylvester broke the silence. "It is true, Sven, that Walter has limited experience as a creative writer. But I have been working with him in the past week, and he has made a great deal of progress. Now, I haven't discussed this with the author yet—" he glanced at me, "but considering the political nature of his work, and the urgency that we find ourselves in with the recent ban on books … I'd be willing to *publish* his book, after editing it myself, in order to distribute it among the people." He looked at Sven and the other writers. When Sylvester spoke again, his voice rose with incredible passion, which I hadn't witnessed until then, "Lapin has made art a crime! She has committed genocide! And now she dares abolish the written word! We must keep literature *alive*!" His eyes were ablaze. He turned to me. "What do you say?"

"Yes. When I have completed the book, everyone here can read it."

"By *people*, I don't mean the people in this room. I don't mean the members of ARM. I mean: the *people*. Of *The Nation*."

Walter Cunningham may be a writer. But I am not Walter Cunningham. I'm not a writer; I'm a detective. My talent is solving cases. Sylvester wanted me to write something that people would read? Something that could ... *save* art? I was supposed to expose the creators, not save them! That was my job, what I was being paid to do. This was all happening too fast. And I couldn't—I couldn't take the responsibility. Why me?

"You're hesitating," Sylvester said. "And that's all right, Walter. Think it over."

Sven was out of his seat. He and Sylvester locked eyes. "After all this time! What about my satires, Sylvester? What about your autobiography? Why not publish those?"

"Those are old works, Sven."

"I'll write a satire tonight, Syl. I'll complete an entire collection of short stories in a week that is superior to anything *this* man could ever write! I've talked about writing a book like this for years now!"

"But you never wrote it."

Sven was at a loss for words ... in more ways than one.

"It's just that," Sylvester began, "Walter has a distinct voice that I feel the common person could relate to. We've been writers all our lives, you and I. As have most of us in this room. With Walter just embracing art ... well, maybe others could read his story, see through his eyes, and then they'll be able to see the wrongs of the world. Then *they'll* begin to see the beauty in art."

Sven searched Sylvester's eyes and Sylvester stared

195

back, calmly, without a flinch.

Finally, Sven sat back in his seat with a pugnacious grunt.

Pugnacious. I hope you read this, Sven. I can use big words too.

"So Walter is sharing first today, I presume," Sylvester added calmly, with feigned indifference.

"As I said, it's not ready yet."

"That's what writer's workshop is for, Walter," said Sven. "We help you get ready. Besides," he added, veering his gaze toward Sylvester, "a work of such significance to the movement must be shared."

What I had written until now—the 196 pages of this book—would reveal that I was a detective on a case to bring down the creators. And those pages were right there, in the brown leather briefcase sitting on the round writer's workshop table. How could I get out of this? I turned to Sylvester for help, but he looked away.

"Isn't that right, Syl?" Sven asked. "Tell Walter he has to share."

I began picking at the arm of my chair.

"Sven is right, Walter," Sylvester said, unable to look in my direction.

I put the briefcase on the table. Touched my index fingers against the cool golden tabs. Began to push against them …

"I can't do it." I dropped by hands to my sides. "It's not ready. Sylvester told me to come to him when I was ready to begin writing and I did. Trust me to do the same this time."

Sylvester took a long breath and his old eyes searched mine. "Although I've seen you writing, you haven't permitted me to read it." Then, in a raised, disappointed voice, as if scolding a child, he continued, "If you want to be invited back into writer's workshop, Walter, you *must* share with us next time."

"Yes, Sylvester."

As writer's workshop came to a close, Sylvester asked me to remain. As the writers left through the room, they looked at me differently. They gave looks of awe, respect, jealousy. At first, I couldn't understand why, but then I realized that it was because of the book I was writing for them, for the movement ... for myself. This was what I wanted, I thought. This was why I wanted the badge.

Sylvester put his hands together and rested them on the table. "What was that about Simon's kid?"

Images flashed through my mind. Memories that I had hidden too far that I couldn't reach inside and pull out. "There was a beggar child—" I stopped.

"Sorry," Sylvester said. "You don't have to tell me. What I wanted to suggest is that you read a chapter from my autobiography. It will give you some context about art and history. Chapter eight, if you will."

"Sure. I'll read it right now."

"Thanks, Walter." What had I done to deserve his trust?

I got out of my seat, picked up the briefcase, and walked to the door. "Oh, and I have something for you ..." he said. I turned around. He reached into his pocket and pulled out some sort of silver writing device with a sharp, metal tip.

"This is an engraver. Since your notebook is made of wood, I thought you could use this to write your title. Have you thought of it yet?"

"Not yet."

"It will come to you. And here, " he said, tossing an apple underhand across the room. I caught it with my right hand.

"For you to taste knowledge. Like Adam did. ARM

is your Eden now."

He smiled as he handed me the engraver.

"I can't write it, Sylvester."

"Yes, you can. Lauren didn't get as far as you."

"Lauren?"

"Don't you know? She started to write a book about the propaganda of The Nation like you, which she wanted the people to read. You two were close. What happened to her, if you don't mind me asking?"

"She's gone ..." I wasn't ready to talk about her, the guilt was too great, my entire being convulsing at the images of her that terrible afternoon. Worst of all was the thought I couldn't get out of my head, as much as I pushed it deep into the burrows of my brain, beneath the nanotrons that had left their shadows in my skull. This thought returned in my dreams; it followed memories, which clung to me at unforeseen moments under the desultory sun:

Could I have known? Could I have saved her?

"I lost someone dear to me, too," Sylvester said. "The love of my life. We all experience loss. It's how we deal with tragedy that defines us. I think it's great that you're writing this book. Writing is the only positive way I know to release my emotions."

"Thank you, Sylvester."

"You're welcome, Walter. You know, my wife is not the only one I lost ..." Sylvester hesitated. He looked at me, and I remembered how he had given me that strange, half-recognizing stare the first time he saw me, crouching beside the compartment of wires, and I thought about how he had requested me to interview him, and for a moment, I thought that Sylvester was about to tell me why. But instead, all he said was, in a soft, languishing, and pained voice, "A man can have all the courage in the world and at the same time none at all."

I entered into the silence of the reading room. Its musty smell no longer reminded me of old tales but instead, I thought of the knowledge kept in these books, yearning to be discovered. As I walked toward the couch as slowly as I could, I spotted a book on one of the tables. Something about it drew me in: maybe its dusty, faded cover, how it looked older than all the other books, its pages yellower, or how it was small enough to fit in the palm of my hand. I read the two words that melted into the cover, *Diamond Sutra*. I leafed through it, opening to the last page, and read:

> Thus shall you think of this fleeting world:
> A star at dawn, a bubble in a stream,
> A flash of lightning in a summer cloud,
> A flickering lamp, a phantom, and a dream.

I flipped to the first page. There was an orange post-it with a silver scribble that I recognized as Sylvester's messy handwriting. He wrote, "the first book, 868 A.D." Wow. The first book ever written.

I wanted to read it but seeing Sylvester's scrawl reminded me of his own book. So I closed *Diamond Sutra*, gently placing it back on the table, and turned to the bookshelf. I pulled out Sylvester's book, feeling the roughness of its dark cover. I sat in the auburn couch and opened to the table of contents:

Chapter Eight: Meeting Weinstein & the Lapin Massacre

I flipped to the chapter and read.

Chapter Twenty: How It Came to Be

Leo Weinstein looked smaller in person. He was hardly five feet tall. That's why his enemies called him the "Jewish Napoleon". I could tell, however, that Leo Weinstein was not a man to be reckoned with. He had deep, brown eyes, thick, heavy eyebrows, a short beard, and an oval-shaped, bald head. As he shook my hand, he looked into my eyes with the kind of self-assurance and resolve that you only see in those rare men who are determined to change the world.

"It's very good to meet you, Mr. Huppington."

"Likewise, Mr. Weinstein. Have a seat."

He locked eyes with me for another moment and then paused, as if the words he were about to utter were the most important in the entire world. Perhaps they were.

"I think you know why I'm here. President Lapin's policies have torn our nation apart. By funneling money into World War III, she caused The Collapse. Our economy may never fully recover. There's also her inexorable alliance with the corporations. The gap between the rich and poor is greater than ever. The unification of church and state. This is the time for change. Despite your ties to Lapin, I know you didn't vote for her. We could use a man like you. Join me and the Equalatic Party, Mr. Huppington. And you will do what is right for your nation."

"And how do you plan on overthrowing the President, Mr. Weinstein? Through acts of violence? Terrorism?"

"There is no other way."

"I do not condone violence of any kind."

"What about her blaming the economy on minorities? Who says she won't do what Hitler tried to do to the Jews?"

"It could never happen."

"But it nearly did! You will be preventing violence by joining us!"

"Gandhi, from the same era as Hitler, once said, 'An eye for an eye makes the whole world blind.' Why not fight back with passive resistance? It is as effective as it is idealistic."

"Do not be naïve. Lapin is looking for scientists capable of developing a new kind of bomb that could wipe out the entire planet. If the Islamic terrorists continue to defeat us in Europe, there is no doubt in my mind that she will not hesitate to use it."

"With the advent of technology in the past 150 years," Weinstein continued, in a speech no doubt rehearsed, "humans have become more and more removed from the society we once knew. It began with television and then the Internet. Then those little black boxes people carried around that gave us access to the Internet at all times, and no one needed to socialize, let alone think. Then the iPhones turned into MiniAs and eventually the chips in our brains. It is true that humans have relied on technology since they invented the spear. But it is only recent inventions that have caused human beings to remove themselves from society and then join another world, which can seem so much better than the real one. This was how UNICE was born. How else would an amalgamation of the Internet, virtual reality, and the human mind be created? I've always said that if you can remove something manmade and society can't function, then we have reached a tipping point. Add a corrupt government to the mix and I hate to say it, but the world may have an end in sight. A bomb, Sylvester. In the hands of Lapin. Can you imagine the consequences?"

A bomb that could wipe out the entire planet? The restrictions on air flight, the cyber security on UNICÉ … could it have actually happened? Is it possible that our nation is the only place in existence? How could we know for sure, without any contact from the outside world? Is there something so ingrained in our mindset that we can't see beyond ourselves, our families, The Nation? I refused to believe that any human was capable of launching a weapon that would destroy all of humankind.

Despite all I had seen, there was still a side that clung to me like a magnet, insisting the truth wasn't true.

The reason for the gap between the rich and poor, the unification between church and state—these were caused by President Lapin. But Lapin wasn't the only one to blame. And neither were the TPF, who carried out her orders. No. It's easy to blame someone else— it's human instinct. But the fact is, we had voted Lapin to power. It was the fault of the people.

"Because of the economy, funding for art programs has been stripped!" I proclaimed. "If I choose to oppose Lapin and we lose, Huppington Books will be terminated."

"But we won't lose!" He looked at me with such fury, such vitality, that the room nearly shook with the sound of his voice. "With the entire Equalatic Party, the Beggars, the lower class, and the middle class unified into a single force—this is the strongest opposition to Lapin there has been since she was elected. She's taken over all branches of the government! It is nothing short of dictatorship!" His eyes were ablaze, his eyebrows reaching to the lines across his forehand. This was a man of passion.

The door to my office swung open, and my seven-year-old daughter skipped into the room. She was holding a book in her hand.

"Daddy! I did it!" She hopped right on my lap. "I read the whole book!"

"Great job! This looks like a difficult book."

"My teacher said that it's at a very high level. That if I work hard, I can be reading the same books as the other kids."

"You have to work very hard. Harder than the other kids."

"Oh, I will, Daddy! You'll see. I'll do it for you! And," she said, reaching into her pocket, "look at my sculpture!" She had built a small sculpture of a man out of wire.

"Very good! Who is that?"

"It's you, silly!"

"It looks just like him," Weinstein said, a little too seriously. She looked at him, as if she had just realized he were in the room.

"Daddy is in a meeting now, sweetheart," I said. "Why don't you go with my secretary to deliver an important package for me."

"What is it?"

"It's a book for Daddy's business. Go to Mary now. She'll take you there."

"Okay!" Iryna replied, jumping off my lap. "Bye!" she waved timidly at Weinstein before leaving the room.

"She seems very smart."

"She has a learning disability, Mr. Weinstein."

"Well, she's certainly creative. Do you think she'll be able to do sculpture in a future with Lapin?"

"Art will never die," I responded. "I wish you all the luck in the world, but I cannot help you. I will not fight violence with violence."

An hour passed and Iryna had not returned. I heard the voice of Weinstein out my window, booming and tempestuous, amplified from Granite Point in the Great

204

Slum. And then I heard shots. Countless explosions in the air, that lasted for minutes, but felt much, much longer. I threw on my jacket and swung open my office door, afraid that I would lose the second woman of my life.

As soon as I opened the door, Iryna fell into my arms. She was crying.

"Oh, thank God you're safe," I held her against my chest. "I'll never let you go again. Not after what happened to Mommy."

"Mary got shot, Daddy! I saw the water hit her chest, and then her heart spill out."

"I can't believe you had to see that."

"We need to save her!"

"There's nothing we can do now."

"I hid from them. The shooters. And then I kicked one in the leg. The one who shot Mary."

"You did what?"

"I kicked him. Because he shot her. He just laughed at me!"

"You shouldn't have done that, Iryna! Next time, you run away, you hear? Violence is never the answer."

———

The Lapin Massacre has been covered up to this very day. Two hundred protestors were killed and the National Uprising was squelched. Although Weinstein escaped, he was found months later and shot for all to see on UNICÉ. Using Weinstein as a scapegoat, Lapin began a sweeping propaganda campaign to turn the people against minorities. She persuaded the people that they were to blame for The Economic Collapse and so we rioted throughout The Nation. The minorities either went into hiding or fled, and from then on, the only people seen were of white, Christian descent. This became known as "The Purge".

Around the same time, Lapin claimed victory in World War III. No one would attack us again, she proclaimed. Her first act was to restrict travel out of the country. I tried to contact some colleagues in Europe but found that UNICE had been censored. Even more mysteriously, they never tried to contact me. To my shock, people did not revolt. They seemed to accept that the rest of the world was not of our concern or at least they pretended to. By then, they had no choice.

I never felt right during that period of my life. It was as if I had failed not only my country, but also myself. I couldn't get that day out of my mind. I could have joined Weinstein, stood up for what was right, instead of being a slave to Lapin, a mindless drone like so many others.

Three months later, James Shields, a rock musician, posted songs on UNICE, calling Lapin a "despot". Days after they were released, they disappeared. As a result, Lapin made all "art", whether it be painting, music, creative writing, etc., illegal and punishable by death.

When Lapin outlawed art, I saw it as an opportunity for redemption. I contacted writers I had published, musicians who were friends with Shields. Art could never die, I knew, and that thought helped me keep faith. I made a promise to myself. I would create a place where people could practice their religions, their cultures, and their art freely.

And so began the creation of the Art Resistance Movement.

Two small hands grabbed my nanojacket and pulled me off the couch. So engrossed in Sylvester's book, I couldn't register who grabbed me until I was thrown against the bookshelf. With her black-and-white bandana inches from my face, Iryna Huppington was staring up at me with her sharp, hazel eyes.

"My father may trust you, Walter. But I don't." I

could have thrown her on the ground in an instant. I didn't think that would be a good idea though.

"What is this book you're writing?"

"Could you let go of me?"

"When you finish that book, give it to me first. Then to my father. Got it?"

"Got it. Please. You're crumpling up my jacket."

She let go. "You mean your *cop* uniform?" she quipped. She examined my face. "Are you wearing *makeup?*"

I put a hand to my cheek. Some of the spray particles were chipping off my face.

"Oh. I was putting on some brown solution, but then decided against getting an artificial tan."

"Uh huh," she said with a smirk. Then she looked down at the floor and up at me. Her eyes looked glossy, like when she pointed her gun at me the day she killed Lester, and I could see a small veil of water forming between her iris and the lens of her eye. "You know you're putting your wife in danger by writing this book of yours. Have you told her about it?"

"I don't think it's any of your business—"

"Well, don't you think you should tell her?" she asked, ignoring my response. "You do realize the danger you're putting her in."

"What do you want, Iryna?"

She shot me a look of contempt. Then she walked to Sylvester's autobiography, which had landed face down on the floor. She picked it up and looked at the page I was reading. "Did you read from any other parts of this book?"

"Not yet."

She studied my face. "Do you think you'll understand my father after reading his book?"

"I don't pretend to."

"Because you won't. You can read about my mother's death. But only I know how much it crushed him." She said it almost matter-of-factly. "He was never the same after that. He loved her as much as any man could love a woman."

"I'm sorry."

She tossed the book back on the couch. "I don't want you reading any more of this," she ordered.

"If you say so."

"Don't be smart with me." She lifted her button-down flannel oversized long-sleeve shirt, exposing a thin stomach with an outie belly button, and a small, black laser pistol. "I can do a lot worse than a kick," she said with a wink.

❦

At night, Anji and I barely said a word to each other. We still had sex, but more out of duty than out of love, as if we were automatrons, trying to fill an absence of emotion. It wasn't the sex though—that was like it always was with those damn sexsuits. It was our lack of communication that was really messing things up. Anji's eyes hardly met mine those days. She'd lock herself in her office and go on UNICÉ. She reconnected with an old friend, she told me, the woman who advised her not to marry me because I didn't make enough money.

The truth was, I had been distant too. The days I spent with Sylvester, the time and energy I put into writing and hiding it from her—all it did was pull us apart. Even when I was with her, my mind was on the book. The drive to write was too great. I wanted so much for Anji to know what I was going through—I wished I could confide in her—but I knew she wouldn't understand. She didn't marry Walter Cunningham.

Then one day, hope prevailed. I'd go into Anji's office and tell her the truth. I was a cop—I could kill a man if I had to. I certainly could talk to my own wife.

It was with this resolve that I came out of the skytrain port and onto the mechanized walkway that led to the triple-decker elevators on the thirty-third floor of the Spiraling Tower. I was coming back from ARM, holding the handle of the briefcase with the manuscript. I watched a pigeon fly into one of the gigantic fans, its feathers taken by the wind in different directions like leaves in an autumn storm. I became lost in thought on how I could describe the pigeons in the book, how they could work as a symbol. It was then that I heard a deep chuckle behind me.

I turned my head slightly to see a TPF officer. I found myself tightening my grip on the handle of the briefcase.

He followed me inside the elevator. I turned to the voice panel and said, "floor eighty-six," and moved to the other side to make room for the TPF officer to select a button. But he remained where he was, standing with his black-rimmed goggles and thick lips facing me. He was going to my floor.

The doors shut. He looked down at my briefcase.

I managed a slight nod of the head at him. He grunted. Why was he going to my floor?!

When we reached the eighty-sixth floor, he moved aside so I could leave the elevator first, and then he stood behind me on the mechanized walkway. I wished I had a weapon. But all I had was the briefcase with the manuscript. I began walking. Then he started to walk behind me. I could hear the weapons clanging against his belt—the liquidators, the missile guns, the mirror-reflective shields. I didn't look back.

When I stepped off the mechanized walkway, I waited for a moment before opening the apartment door. I looked to my left.

"Nice to meet you, neighbor," he remarked and his door opened with a click.

I felt a rush of relief when I came inside the apartment. I imagined myself writing about what had just happened. It would make such a suspenseful scene! But then reality struck. A TPF officer was living next door.

Iryna was right. I had to tell Anji the truth. I had put her in danger and she should know about it. I needed to tell her … for us. But when I got to her office, I could hear her voice through the door, chatting with that friend who never liked me.

"I want to be a part of his life again but he doesn't open up with me. He's always out of the house, or in his office. One time I caught him under our bed! He's acting weird, I'm telling you … No, it's not that. He wouldn't *intentionally* turn Tommy against me. He's just … I think he envies my father. That's why he encouraged Tommy to draw …" I heard a deep, heavy sigh. "I think back to how it came to be, our marriage … I know we loved each other once. But now, I just don't know anymore."

That hit me hard. I walked back into the hall, her words penetrating my skull. The saddest thing of all wasn't what Anji said though. It was that she couldn't be open with me. I took a deep breath as I came into my office, trying to come to terms with … what she really thought. Our connection was too strong for too long; there must be a way to make things better. I wanted my wife back. But it takes more courage to tell the truth to someone you love than to lie.

I went back to the desk in my office and stared out

the oval window, daring myself to look into the sun.
I couldn't write. Everyone can see the sun out of the
corner of their eye but no one can look directly at it.
When I walked through the Slums, ate dinner, or did
anything *but* write, ideas would appear. Yet as I sat at
my desk, staring at the blank pages of my manuscript,
I couldn't write a thing. The sun was too strong.

It was too much responsibility. Sylvester wanted
millions of people to read this. I went onto UNICÉ to
get my mind off the book. I thought I'd turn on a movie.
I watched a few minutes of the new Richard Pellman
action flick that was showing in the Entertainment
District. He was firing his liquidator at a group of
Beggars who were viscously attacking him. He killed
them all, of course, and then stood up as straight as
an autamotron and stated, "I win again. You can never
beat me." It was so obvious to me that he was acting. I
couldn't believe I had liked him before; it was clear he
had no talent. So what if he made a lot of money and
was famous? Those things don't make a man happy. I
even found myself feeling bad for the guy. Here he was,
being seen by everyone and making a fool of himself. I
looked down at the manuscript. I was just an ordinary
man. I was no Richard Pellman.

"Message. From The Chief."

The Chief. Just hearing that mechanized voice utter
"The Chief" gave me a terrible knot in my stomach.
I thought about what Sylvester had written about
Weinstein, how he had felt guilty for not joining him
when he had the chance, and how that sense of guilt drove
him to create ARM. It was the feeling that had overcome
Lauren and crushed her. I didn't want it to crush me.
But how could I consider myself a true member of ARM
when I couldn't tell them who I really was?

"Have you gotten into the weapons facility?" asked

the Chief in his smoke-stained voice. "The TPF were here. They want to take Huppington to trial. I'm giving you three more days to get that evidence, Victor, or I'm putting someone else on the case, and you won't come within inches of a detective badge."

I laughed. Detective badge? Bring Huppington to trial? There was no such thing as "evidence." But then I stopped laughing. The TPF weren't going to bring Huppington to trial. I had given them the location of the underground lair. They were coming to ARM.

Chapter Twenty-One: The Raid

Briefcase in hand, I walked down the wet, limestone hallway, where the music hovering in the air sounded out of tune, the smell of incense overbearing, and the prayers lugubrious. The faces of the creators ... wait. Why haven't I been capitalizing this? The faces of the Creators walking in and out of the hallway were drawn with oblivious smiles. More than once I thought I heard the whirring of helicopters and found myself looking back toward the winding stairwell. I had to tell Sylvester the truth. I had to tell the Creators who I really was, what I had done, and that the TPF were on their way. Or else I'd never be able to live with myself.

But when I walked into writer's workshop, the seat next to Sylvester, where I composed much of this manuscript, was occupied by Iryna Huppington. She had a small sheet of paper in front of her and her eyes moved up and down the page. Vivek sat beside her. Maybe they were there because they knew about the raid already, and I wouldn't have to tell them who I really was.

I leaned against the wall behind them. Sara, who came in last, stood by my side, and said, "I just want to say that you were right. This isn't a place for kids." I wondered if I really was right. "Simon's with him. I do wish he came to writer's workshop. We have someone else who can take care of him. But he insistit that he wanted to stay with the baby today." She looked down at the briefcase, which I had placed between the wall and the heels of my feet.

"Is it finisht?" she asked. She leaned her arm into mine.

"Not yet. I haven't been able to write the past couple days."

"Writer's block."

"What?"

"The most important thin' with writer's block is to never stop writin'. That's the worst thin' you can do. If you can't think, just write anything, and ventually, it'll turn into somethin' you can use."

"Thanks for the advice," I said, but I wasn't fully listening. Iryna kept studying the crumpled sheet of paper as if she were preparing for a speech and Sylvester was looking around to get everyone's attention.

"As you can see," Sylvester began, "my daughter has written something that she wants to read to all of you. Iryna?"

She looked at her father. "This is for *you*," she said. She held up the piece of paper and read:

"Thou art a leader, a rebel, a sinner,
a sardine in a sea of sharks.
Thou art a follower, a conformist, a saint,
aiming a slingshot at a lit cannon.

Thou art searching for a man lost behind
yet the answer is in front of your tired eyes.
Forgive yourself, make peace—
so that you ascend to a better place."

Iryna got out of her chair and wrapped her arms

around her father in a long, tight embrace. She gave him one last squeeze and then looked into his face. Sylvester whispered, through glassy eyes, "You're right, Iryna. Thank you. I'll do it later." And he looked at *me*.

Before I could figure out what Iryna's poem was about, how it could make her hug her father like that, or what Sylvester was going to "do" to me later—I got a message from The Chief. I mirrored it from the nanotrons to my eyes and heard urgency in his voice:

"The TPF are coming. Get out while you can."

I looked at the writers. Their notebooks were all different. Sven's was a yellow, business-like pad; Sara's was small enough that it could fit snugly in her pocket; Sylvester's was a one-subject notebook with blue lines and sharp silver ink, the same color as his hair, which took over the page in an unintelligible scribble. What would happen if a policeman spotted one of those notebooks hidden underneath their coat, or if they dropped it on the floor of the skytrain? If these writers' husbands or wives or children found their notebook hidden in their closet, how would they explain the danger they had put their family in? They risked everything for their art.

I listened to the jotting of pens. I watched Vivek take Iryna's small hand and gently hold it in his. I looked at Sylvester, the deep crevices under his eyes, the wrinkles in his face, the way he smiled at his daughter.

"We need to get out of here."

All heads turned to me.

"You're in danger. We need to leave."

"I'm sorry, Walter?" Sylvester asked.

"It's not Walter. My name is Victor. Detective Victor Vale."

The room went silent. Sven peered into my eyes and

the corners of his mouth twitched, spreading into a wide grin. Sara looked me up and down and then took a step back, her body and mind moving away from me into a cloud of mistrust. Vivek and Iryna were on their feet, as if ready to take on whatever force was about to enter the room. Sylvester was still, except for a slight nod of the head, as if he knew all along.

"Everythin' you wrote … the *book* …" Sara trailed off.

"I say *dispose* of him!" Sven pronounced. "What is to be done?" He looked at Sylvester. Everyone looked at Sylvester. He frowned, with a glance at Sven and the other writers. He didn't speak, but looked at his notebook as if his writings could somehow tell him what to do. I felt like a defendant on trial, awaiting his sentence.

Finally, he spoke.

"What Victor has done is inexcusable. He exposed us to the police. Because of him, we have been discovered. But Victor did not have to reveal his true identity. It takes courage to tell someone who you really are."

I remembered what Sylvester said to me after giving me that apple, "A man can have all the courage in the world and at the same time none at all." There was something Sylvester wanted to tell me that day but he couldn't find the courage to say it.

Sven widened his eyes, staring at Sylvester, and his mouth hung open. Then he turned his head to me, slowly, his eyes flickering, as if he had just thought of something disgusting yet irresistible. "Let's finally see your *book*, detective. Or is it a police report?"

Sven got out of his seat and walked abruptly to me, earlobes flapping, and before I realized what he was doing, he leaned down, reaching his hands between my legs to grab the handle of the briefcase. I clutched it from behind, and we pulled both ways as if we were children in a game of tug of war. Sven spun the numbers of the gold dials with his left hand, trying to break the code; my grip was getting looser, and I could feel it slipping away—

With a karate chop, Vivek knocked the briefcase to the floor. It fell to the ground and opened.

Vivek picked up my notepad. "This is book," he said, his blue eyes meeting mine.

Sven snatched it out of Vivek's hands. "Look here!" he exclaimed. He read, "'Not long after the Cleansing Act, I was promoted to Detective ... I didn't care about creators'!" Then he ripped out the first pages of my manuscript and let them drop to the floor. They floated into the air, landing in different parts of the room. They were picked up and read and there was nothing I could do.

"In times like these, we MUST work together!" Sylvester shouted with incredible forcefulness. The room seemed to reverberate with the sound of his voice. "We are about to be raided!!" Sylvester pounded his fist on the table and looked up at me with desperation. His tone was powerful and the room went silent once again.

The silence was broken by two shots of a laser pistol. Then screaming, feet running, an indiscriminate bang of a fallen object. Then I heard it—the pounding of black, leather boots against the limestone floor, its echo getting louder. Iryna, Vivek, and Sven had their laser pistols out and ready. The echo of the boots faded away, and then it was quiet, the air as still as the wind before a hurricane, and the writers looked with dread at the door, as its old-fashioned knob began to turn.

The door swung open, and Iryna, Vivek, and Sven fired. The crisscrossing of the lasers lit up the room as the TPF officer hit the ground face first, his goggles cracking against the floor, and his gun-ridden belt hitting the ground with a smack. I leapt onto the floor, crawled under the table, pushing my body to the pages of my manuscript. One was leaning casually against a wall, another was stuck under the TPF officer, and a third had found a home between Sven's feet. I seized the page against the wall and reached between Sven's shoes to see his hand snatch the page away. He held it in front of me with a sly smile. I was ready to take it from him, fight him for it if I had to. But he placed it in my hands.

I turned the TPF officer on his back so I could pull out the third page of my manuscript, and as I did, I heard a scream. I looked up at Sara, who was staring at the young face of the TPF officer in horror. It was Simon.

I noticed Sven holding a liquidator in his right hand. I gazed around the room and saw that Simon had been stripped of his weapons; Iryna and Sven had taken them. I felt for a weapon in my nanojacket even though I knew I hadn't brought one. And then I looked down and felt the pages in my hands. I had seen the TPF officer with a belt full of weapons, and I hadn't taken one. I had gone for the manuscript instead.

I could hear the TPF coming closer. Sara was kneeling by Simon's side, crying, holding onto him as if he were a lifeboat.

"You have to leave him," I commanded.

"Why should I listen to *you*?"

"All you can do now is save yourself." I put out my hand. "For your son." She looked at me suspiciously. And she took my hand. I pulled her up from the ground.

That was when I heard him gasping for air. Sylvester

was reaching his arms out, his eyes lost in a daze. He tried to hold onto the table but his grip wasn't strong enough and his fingers slipped, disorientation seizing him as the front of his head hit the edge of the table and he fell backward to the floor.

Iryna took her bandana and wrapped it around his bleeding forehead. "I'll get you out of here," she said. "You'll be okay." Sylvester gave her a faraway look. I felt a heavy nudge on my shoulder and turned to see Vivek looking down at me.

"We help him," he said. As I approached Sylvester, he gave me a sudden look of recognition. I put his arm on my shoulder and lifted him up with Vivek on the other side. We dragged him to the door, Iryna by my side, the writers following us with their eyes. I looked at the empty table, where I had left my briefcase, and saw that Sara was holding it.

Sven walked in front of us as we came out into the chaos of the hallway and the sulfuric smell of the liquidators drifted through my nose. Amid the TPF officers stomping through the main entrance, the Creators running in and out of doors, and the frenzied shots in the air, I saw Ralph's yellow butterfly, with the black spots along its back, darting through the hallway. It flew inches above the floor before plummeting back to the ground, its wing still broken. Then a black boot rose and fell, and crushed the butterfly beneath it.

Sven shot at the officer and I turned to face the back entrance. Sara ran in front of us and pulled open the door that led to a stairwell while Sven remained behind. I could feel the pressure of Sylvester on my back as we carried his large body up the stairs. He was breathing heavily by my ear and would turn his head and look at Vivek or me, utter the words "so much ..." and then his head would fall to his chest.

When we reached the archive of paper books, Sylvester mumbled in a barely audible voice, "Put me down."

"No, father," Iryna said.

"I said put me down!"

"All right Dad, but we're going to get you a doctor."

We put Sylvester down slowly, on the wooden floor, and his head rested against a shelf of dusty books. Some of the blood from his forehead had seeped through Iryna's bandana. He took a deep breath and looked relieved.

"We can 'scape from here," Sara said, looking at the door that led into the street.

"Take this," Iryna said to her, taking out her gun, "And get Sylvester a doctor."

"I go instead," Vivek said. "Must fight. I return with doctor. She is young. Has child. Must escape."

Vivek opened his arms and Iryna fell into them, a tear running down her cheek. He gave her a long, passionate kiss. Then he turned to Sara, said, "go," and plodded back down the stairs.

Sara hesitated by the door. "Get out of here!" I shouted. She looked at me, Iryna, and Sylvester, then put my briefcase on the floor, opened the door, and ran.

Sylvester gave a look of discomfort and rubbed his left arm.

"You're gonna make it," I said even though I didn't know if I believed it.

"You'll be okay, Dad," Iryna said. "A doctor is coming."

"So much ... " he began to say again, " ... *violence*. What have I done?"

"I'm sorry," I said. "I caused this." I felt as if I were going to cry.

"No, you didn't, Victor," said Sylvester. "And I am

sorry. You have courage." He took Iryna's hand … and mine. He pulled us toward him.

"I hope," he said, his words fading to a whisper, "that my children will lead ARM."

My mind went blank. I couldn't speak. Reality flashed before me and I looked at Sylvester as if I were outside my own dream. I lifted my hand. Pointed to my chest.

"Yes," Sylvester said. I looked at him as he said that, and it felt as if I were looking into a mirror at myself.

"Forgive us, Victor," Iryna said.

"We?"

She nodded her head.

"I'm so proud of you," Sylvester said, looking at Iryna.

"Daddy!" Iryna shouted in the same voice as the seven year old who showed her father a metal sculpture that she created in his image. Sylvester looked at Iryna, then at me, and I could see a slight smile on his face, his eyes curving upward, forming a smile of their own. Then he gave that faraway look again, and I could feel his hand slipping out of mine. His head leaned against the bookshelf and specks of dust fell onto his shoulders. His eyes closed.

Nothing was real anymore. I left the archive. Returned to the hallway. Shots whizzed by me. I didn't care. I had to know the truth.

I went to the reading room. Pulled out Sylvester's autobiography.

Chapter Five: The Biggest Mistake of My Life

She was an angel and a poet. She wrote about tennis, money, and sunsets. She was as innocent as a child and as sweet as an apple. I told her she was my favorite intern. I told her I liked her writing. I told her to stay after work one moonlit afternoon. Then I crushed her angel's wings.

She didn't love me. We were using each other. Then the impossible happened. She got pregnant. I tried to convince her not to have it. She was so young. In the back of my head, I knew that my reputation would be tarnished. She wanted to put him up for adoption. It was a good solution.

Then I found myself wanting him. I had no one and he was a part of me. But then I realized that I was young too. I wasn't ready to care for a child.

I put down the book. Walked back into the hallway and for a moment, I just stood there, listening to the screams, the stomping of the black leather boots, waiting for one of the bullets to hit me. Why should I care what happens to me? Nobody else did. Sylvester had titled the chapter, "The Biggest Mistake of My Life."

I felt someone tugging at my arm. It was Iryna. "Let's go!" she shouted and pulled me through the back exit. She closed the door and looked into my eyes.

"He said that the mistake wasn't having you. It was letting you go."

Chapter Twenty-Two: The Remnants of ARM

The Chief's razor collection was in pristine condition. He reassembled the broken razors and then washed, dried, and waxed them. They glistened in the sunlight that shone through the panes of his window. They were as shiny as The Chief's exuberant smile.

"We've taken down the Creators!" He put out his hand. I looked at the rings on his fingers, the purple veins that reached from his knuckles to his wrist. I shook it.

"So happy, you're speechless?" he asked, walking to his collection of razors. He looked out the window at the wide steps that led into the station. "I guess I can die now," he said with a chuckle. He reached for the comb. He picked it up gingerly and looked into the mirror. "My son always knew the importance of appearance." I thought I could see a tear in his eye. "But he was also *good*." He put the comb back on the top shelf and picked up a razor with an herb-scented blade. "You know, I didn't buy all these razors," he said with a hint of guilt. "Some of them I designed. Put together myself." He put the blade to his nose, took a sniff, and put it down.

He came back to his desk, ruffled through his top drawer, pulled out a roll of bills, and the detective badge.

He placed them in my hands.

"You've earned it," he said.

I looked down at the golden eagle, traced the silver letters of the word "DETECTIVE" with the tips of my fingers, felt the weight of it in the palm of my hand. I felt the rough texture of the green paper, gazed at the zeros on each bill.

I couldn't remember what it was all for.

As I left The Chief's office, I received a message from Iryna:

"I need to see you."

Light seeped through small round bullet holes in the tall purple doors of Huppington Books. The voice recognition box had been smashed. There was no one to let me inside. There was no invisible force to pull open the doors.

Huppington Books had been destroyed. Automatrons lay lifeless on the floor. The three-dimensional books on the walls looked somehow faded. The wires that lined the floor and led into the small compartment behind the automatrons' desks had been cut into pieces of what looked like red and green confetti. If only the automatron secretary hadn't reached out her hand to save me and it was I who had touched that wire instead.

Standing there, as if an extension of the room itself, was Iryna. She hadn't washed her bandana-less hair and dirty clumps had formed around her scalp. Her back and shoulders slumped, as if her body was admitting defeat. She looked small.

"Wow. Look at you," she gazed into my face, studying the features of Victor Vale. "I'm so glad you came." Her voice started to waver and she tried to control it. "Vivek ..." Her face crumbled before my eyes and she began to cry.

"He didn't make it."

"It'll be okay."

She looked up at me, her hazel eyes trapped behind veils of water. Then she gave me a slight smile and went for a hug. I held up my hand. I demanded an explanation.

"If you knew who I was," I glared down at her, feeling the coming of fury through clenched teeth, "why did you treat me like that? Right from the start, you made things difficult for me."

"I'm sorry. I have been an icicle, cold and unforgiving."

"Stop hiding behind your similes and metaphors! You're just like Da...*Sylvester*, I mean. He could only express how he felt through his writing. Well, I'm a detective and I tell it straight. Your father wasn't man enough to tell his son the truth."

"Do you feel better," she asked, a crack in her voice, "now that you've let off some steam?"

"A little. 'Thou art searching for a man lost behind / yet the answer is in front of your tired eyes.' These were the words from your poem to him. You never wanted him to tell me, did you?"

"I envied you. How you appeared suddenly after all this time and seeing the attention Dad gave you ... my whole life I thought *I'd* be the head of ARM. Forgive me."

"You'll always be their leader. Now let's go inside."

I followed her slumped back into Sylvester's office. It was in shambles. His desk had been overturned, smashed. His chair was ripped and a leg was broken. The only thing undamaged was the painting that covered the entrance to ARM; it had been put right back in its place. I wanted to reach into that painting, grab Lapin by the neck, and strangle the life out of her until she begged for forgiveness. But vengeance can't bring back the dead.

Iryna looked down at my empty hands. "Where is it?"

"It's under the floorboards beneath my bed. It's not finished yet."

The door to Sylvester's office smacked against the wall and fell off its hinges. The TPF officer who I had spoken to in The Chief's office stomped into the room, with two other officers, and behind them … was Kenneth.

"Hello, Detective Vale," said the TPF officer. "My good friend, Kenneth—I think you know him? He told me you'd be back here after the raid. That you had become one of *them*. I didn't believe him—at the station, you told me what I needed to know and now your job is done—but well, here you are."

"Quite the opposite," I replied, glaring at Kenneth. "My job is to serve The Nation by turning over the Creators. Some escaped yesterday. I have returned to finish them off. I never leave a job undone."

"Have him *kill* her!" exclaimed Kenneth. "That'll show where his allegiance really lies!"

"Did you *speak*?" The TPF officer turned to face Kenneth.

"I was just suggesting—"

"I am in charge here. You have led me to them. Now you may go."

"But—"

"That's an *order*!"

Kenneth grimaced. But then his expression changed. That mischievous smile slowly formed. "Revenge, Victor. It's a relief. To finally get *justice*." And then with a long, deep sigh, he left.

"*So*," the TPF officer said, leering at Iryna, "you must

be Sylvester's daughter. I was expecting better." Iryna's face turned to stone. She opened her mouth and spat into the officer's face. I could feel myself smile.

The officer wiped away the spit with his arm and pulled out his missile gun. I reached my hand into my pocket to pull out my liquidator but two hands grabbed me from behind.

"So Kenneth was right," the TPF officer said. "These Creators can so easily corrupt. They are by nature selfish beings. What makes what you do so special? Why can't you contribute to society like the rest of us?"

"And what's your contribution, exactly?" Iryna quipped. "Killing innocent people for power? You'll always be kissing Lapin's dirty feet."

He pointed his gun at Iryna's face. "You know, it's really a shame," he said. "If you grew out your hair and got a boob job, you'd be a fine piece of meat." I struggled to free myself from the officers' grips but they were too strong. "Alas, you'll have to join the rest of them. Goodbye."

The missile spun out of his gun. In a millisecond, my mind flashed an image of Iryna's eyes shutting, a feeling of hopeless guilt formed around me, my arms struggling to break free. And then the missile went between her eyes, through her small, thick skull, through the back of her occipital lobe, and out the window. The glass shattered and I kicked the officer who held me in the knee, elbowed him in the stomach, whipped out my liquidator and shot the TPF officers in the head: one, two, and three. They fell to the ground like dark vanishing shadows, puddles of blood seeping onto the floor. Iryna was shaking. I went to hold her but my hands went through her body. Despite what I had just seen, I had forgotten that she was a hologram.

A moaning came from the floor. It was the TPF

officer; I had shot him in the neck and he was still alive. I stepped toward the sound and took out my liquidator.

"This is for Lauren," I said.

"Wait," he replied. He was struggling to speak. Something in his tone compelled me to hear his last words:

"Lapin's an automatron."

What in hell—

It couldn't be.

I pointed it at his face and looked away as I pulled the trigger.

"He's gone now," I said. Iryna gave a shudder and stared into nothingness.

"We need to get out of here. Where did you transmit from?"

She stared absently at the dead officers.

"Snap out of it!" I yelled. "Where did you transmit from?" Her gaze shifted to behind Huppington's desk and at the painting, meeting the eyes of Lana Lapin.

Iryna walked ahead of me, taking slow steps down the winding stairwell. When we reached ARM, the limestone hallway was eerily silent. The bodies had been removed but the stench of death remained. The religion room was empty except for scrolls that had been torn to pieces and left lying on the floor. The medley of chants and smell of incense were replaced with a bereaved absence, as if God had deserted the earth and had gone to seek a more worthy species. The colorful door that led into the virtual world was stained with blood. The heads of each and every sculpture had been blown off. The door to the free sex room looked lonely without the moans of pleasure coming from inside. The giant canvas in the art room was filled with bullet holes and broken instruments lined the floor. The chairs that formed a circle in the political discussion room had been tossed aside in a state of anarchy. As I looked at all the wreckage, I wondered if the Creators would ever come back here. Or if they'd abandon it forever, like a forgotten child.

We came to the solid granite door, with the silver numbers on the side, 0–9, and Iryna told me to wait. Her image melted away. Moments later, I could hear the clicking of the deactivation devices, the door buzzed, and Iryna walked into the hall. She hugged me, her little arms pushing against my back, her head resting on my shoulder. I thought about George, how we could look into each other's eyes and know what the other was thinking. There was a familial bond between us that I had with no one else as a child, an unspoken understanding, and we didn't even share the same blood. As I held Iryna's small body in mine, I shut my eyes and thanked God for my sister.

She held onto me for a moment before letting go. She had lost her lover and her father. I had to put my anger aside and tell her that there was a man in her life, someone to care and protect her.

"I'm here for you, Iryna."

She looked into my eyes, speaking two soft words:

"Thank you."

Then she paused. And asked, "Do you want to know where your mother is?"

"No."

"Okay."

The weapons facility was cold and damp. Narrow tables lined its metal walls. On one of the tables lied various objects: complexion spray cans made from scratch, magnets, digital timers, a solid silver substance in a glass bowl. There were fuses, serrated wires, lasers in glass tubes, wave guns, laser pistols, grenades. On another table were boxes with the picture of a skull with a red X through it and the letters RDD. Beside them were mounds of beige powder in plastic bags with stickers that read SEMTEX-H. At the end of the table were silvery white discs of metal, shaped like large buttons. Uranium. Of all the rooms, the weapons facility, with its deactivation devices, voice recognition, and number code, was the only one that the TPF couldn't enter. It was why they needed me.

"What's the code to get in here?" I asked.

"There never was one. Those numbers were for show—to distract the undercover agents. Only Dad and I had access ... and Sven. Dad imported the solid granite from Europe before the War. That's why the TPF can't break down the door—it's a foreign material. Dad had this section built as a safe haven in case of a raid. It was Sven who began using it to make weapons."

"Why all this trust in Sven?"

"Dad's known Sven for a long time."

What did they plan to do with all these weapons? Although they had enough materials that they could cause some serious damage, the weapons were primitive compared to that of the TPF. If that was whom they wanted to fight, they might as well not even try.

I followed Iryna through the scent of rust to another granite door at the end of the room. Iryna scanned the back of her hand, and the door opened. We came into a small, round room. It was bare except for an HTD in the corner, and twenty or so plastic chairs in a semicircle facing a table. Sitting there were the remaining members of ARM. Sven was present, scribbling furiously in his notebook, and so was Sara, with her son. Iryna and I stood in front of the table and everybody turned to look at us as we entered. Sara widened her wild, gray eyes when she saw me, got out of her seat, and came toward me, her baby cradled in her arms.

"You 'ave brown hair!"

"Yes, I do."

"You look so different. This is my son."

He was squirming in her arms. He looked like Tommy in his first months. I touched his tiny fingers.

Sara smiled at me. "So are you our leader now?"

"Sara," Iryna said, clearing her throat. "Have a seat. We have a lot to talk about." I looked at my sister's face. It was red.

"Yes, indeed," Sven said. He got out of his chair and stood beside us. "The TPF were unable to detect the deactivators of the weapons facility. That is a sign. I've contacted our friends in San Francisco and Austin. They're trying to coordinate a nation-wide revolt. We've been developing these weapons for years. It's time we put them to use. It's time we fought back."

Everyone started talking at once. Yelling over each other, expressing their opinions, nothing getting accomplished. "Quiet!" Iryna shouted. They kept talking. "Silence!" yelled Sven. There was still commotion. I looked into the eyes of each person. A moment later, the room had gone quiet.

Sara, one of the few people who hadn't been talking, hesitantly raised her hand.

"What is it?" Iryna asked.

"Well, if you all wanna fight, that's okay, but I want my son to be safe. Is it true, Iryna, that Vivek built ships?"

"Well, yes, that was his job during the War."

"Did he build anythin'… for *us*?"

There was silence for a moment.

"In fact, there was an electric auto helm that he hid from the TPF in case we ever needed to escape."

"Escape?!" shouted Sven. "I'm surprised at you,

Iryna," he said with a tone of disappointment. He looked around at the others. "We will not give up!"

"I've worked for the enemy." I interjected. All eyes landed on me. "I know how they operate. You can stay and fight if you want. But there's no way in hell that twenty people with dirty bombs and grenades will be able to take down the TPF. It's suicide."

"It's making a statement!" Sven declared. "I'm not a *coward!*"

"They're not going to stop," I said forcefully, glaring into Sven's brown eyes, "until we're all *dead.*"

"I know I can't live with myself if I don't stay and fight." Sven scanned the room. "Many of you lost family because of the Cleansing Act. We must fight back for ethnic identity and religious freedom!"

The remaining members of ARM hummed in approval. Sven smirked. He waited until he had everyone's attention and then he turned to me and said, "*I* make the decisions here—Iryna and I. Not only are you new to ARM but you're a *rat.*"

The room became quiet. They were waiting for me to respond. But I couldn't. He was right. If it weren't for me, none of this would have happened.

"*Walter Cunningham* was a fake," Iryna said. "This man is Victor."

I looked at the faces in front of me. I had to be honest with them. So I said, "Walter Cunningham will always be a part of me."

Sven smiled, that wide, knowing smile. "Sit down, *fink*," he said. "If Sylvester weren't your father, I'd kill you in an instant. I wouldn't even listen to your dying wishes."

Sylvester. That faraway look in his eyes as he slipped away … he abandoned me. I could never abandon my own son. But I did force my will upon Tommy, told him time and time again that he had to be a lawyer, that he had to *choose*. I corrected my mistake—I told him that he should be what *he* wanted to be. And my father—

"*You* sit down," I said to Sven. "My father's dying wish was that his two children lead ARM. Isn't that right, Iryna?"

"It's true."

"So take a seat, Sven. And I *don't* want to kill you. I prefer to work against my enemies and *with* my friends."

"Yeah, Sven," Sara added, "You don't 'ave to be so *opprobrious* all the time."

Sven tried to look defiant by putting his hands to his hips and lifting his head in the air. He turned to Iryna. "Are you with me? You've always fought back. I know that you are the *true* leader of ARM."

Iryna hesitated. She hesitated! How could my own sister even think about turning against me? Then again, she told me she was envious of me usurping her power, and here I was, doing that very thing.

Iryna looked around at the remaining members of the Art Resistance Movement. They watched her with eager expressions, waiting for her reply. How could I convince her that I was right? How could I show her that her father never wanted there to be violence?

I leaned toward her little ear, and whispered, "You don't have to kick."

She gazed into my eyes as if she were looking at someone else.

"My father never supported the building of weapons. He always said that if we used acts of violence, we were no better than *them*."

"But Iryna—" Sven said, "You yourself—"

"Sit down, Sven."

233

Finally, Sven sat down.

"I say we go to Europe," she continued. "Norway. My father went there before the air flight restrictions and said it was the most beautiful place he'd ever seen. Who knows what's there, but it can't be worse than here." She looked at Sven, and added sharply, "This isn't giving up. Before we go, we'll distribute Victor's book. This way we'll fight with words, not violence, like Sylvester would have wanted. Sven, you can stay here if you want with whoever would like to join you. But the rest of us need to get out of here as soon as possible. Let's leave tomorrow at noon. We'll meet at the shipyards. No messages about this on UNICÉ." She turned to me. "And your book? It's finished?"

"It will be. Tonight."

"It has to be," she said. "We have no other choice."

The remaining members of ARM got out of their chairs and went back to their homes. I couldn't imagine the decisions they had to make that night. Whether to stay with Sven and fight or escape with Iryna and me. Which possessions to keep and which to leave behind. To either convince their loved ones to leave with them ... or to give a final kiss goodbye.

I paid a visit to the reading room. Everyone had left ARM already, but I felt an irresistible compulsion to return to the room where I had learned the truth about my father. I had to see if Huppington's biography had somehow survived.

The calm stillness of the reading room had been replaced with a haunted silence. The books on the shelves had been watered, sprayed thoroughly with the TPF's hoses and left soaking in the stoplight red buckets. Pages floated to the top, and all I could make out were the lines and curves of letters blended together in a watery blur. Shakespeare's *Hamlet* lied open on the floor with the mark of a dirty boot. I spotted a small book on a shelf … *Diamond Sutra*. It was torn to shreds. When I tried to pick it up, the shards of paper fell through my fingers, ancient words tumbling to the ground, their meaning lost forever.

I went to the couch where I had left Sylvester's book. Where was it? I stuck my hand into the couch, rummaging my arm through the stickiness of blood on leather, my mind numb to the feeling. My finger brushed against something rough. I reached out and took hold of its dark, rusty cover. I pulled it out. Held it in my hands. I opened it and found what I was looking for, the pages from my father that you have now read. I pulled out those pages, folded them, and put them in my pocket so I could copy them into my book. These pages have been saved.

It was then that I felt another presence in the room. The books seemed to shiver in fright. I felt it so strongly that something inside me told me not to look up, to keep my eyes pointed down on my father's book. But then I heard her voice. It was slow, deliberate, and with such force that I had to lift my eyes. There, standing in front of me, was President Lapin.

Chapter Twenty-Three: The Last Book Ever Written

There was an absence in her eyes. Of all the features that I can recall—the perfectly straight blond hair that outlined her pale face like a yellow arc around the moon, the pointed nose, the thin, hardly visible lips, the hands with veins the color of wine, the curve-less, sexless body, in clothes as plain and white as snow—it was her eyes that I will remember the most. As I looked into them, I sensed a void, an emptiness of emotion, an absence of any form of compassion. Yet at the same time, her charcoal-colored irises controlled me with a laser-like stare. I could tell, with a single glance at those eyes, that what the TPF officer said was true, what Sven knew all along … President Lapin was an automatron.

"Where's the book?"

All I could think about as she spoke, in my state of shock, was how this could have happened. Her metal could have been painted white, that was explicable, but how could an automatron have taken over The Nation? Had she gained control through some sort of egregious human error?

I know that you are doubting this, and I don't blame you. And I can't provide you with the answers—I don't know them. All I can tell you is the thought that entered my head when I first saw her: anything can happen when technology gets out of hand.

"Where's the book, Vale?"

Her lips curled when she spoke, pronouncing each syllable clearly, purposely, monotonously. Standing beside and behind her were a swarm of TPF officers, also holograms, but wearing transmission devices on their gloves so they could point their liquidators at me. They peered at me through their goggles.

I couldn't speak. There she was, President Lapin, in front of my eyes. One of the TPF officers marched toward me, and to my horror, snatched Huppington's book, and tore off its cover. I stood there, helpless, as he ripped up the last remaining book in the reading room, the words my father wrote.

Lapin watched with those empty eyes. It was then that I began to gather the courage I needed to face her. To, somehow, get out of that room alive. I reminded myself that Lana Lapin was an automatron. Humans invented the automatrons … we created her. If we made them, then we could control them. I could control Lapin.

As the TPF officer tore up the pages of the past, I thought about how I could preserve the words of the future. I had to save the manuscript. It's what Sylvester would have wanted.

So I finally managed to utter, "I destroyed it."

She laughed. A shrill, high, laugh that reached the corners of the room, its mockery bouncing off the walls in an unbearable echo.

"Take him."

The TPF officers came toward me, and I knew that this was my last chance.

"Let me explain." If I had spoken loudly, desperately, perhaps Lapin would have let the TPF officers arrest me. But I said it quietly yet firmly, and the simple statement carried with it such crafty confidence that Lapin held up her hand.

"Wait."

I looked into those absent, controlling eyes, and said, "I only wrote the manuscript to convince the terrorists I was one of them. They don't know it, but last night, I sprayed the manuscript with water from my kitchen sink and then soaked it. The pages have been watered. Completely destroyed."

"Search the room," Lapin instructed. The TPF officers surveyed the room, picking out ineligible pages from the buckets, trying to decipher some sort of meaning, turning over the couch behind me without a hint of restraint. I tried not to panic. I repeated to myself: Lapin is an automatron.

"ARM is planning a rebellion against The Nation." I was speaking quickly now. "We're meeting back here tomorrow."

"Take us to the weapons facility," she commanded.

"I can't. There is no code, and I don't have access. They'll be retrieving the weapons tomorrow. We're meeting at noon. Come then. Just leave my family alone. They know nothing of this, I promise you. If I lead you to the Creators, will you do that for me?"

"That depends on if you're telling the truth," said Lapin, not slyly or wicked, but matter-of-factly, as if she were discussing the weather.

"I have and always will be a loyal member of The Nation and to you, President Lapin. The Creators trust me. Spare me tonight and I will lead you to the weapons facility tomorrow. The terrorists will be suspicious if I don't show up. Let me complete the mission I started; let me solve this case. Allow me to help you take down the Creators, once and for all."

"I should take you," Lapin stated. "You killed a TPF

officer. But we will return tomorrow. If you have lied, you and your family will die."

"Thank you, President. It is the honor of my life to meet you and I will serve you always."

I peered one last time into those eyes. Her sexless body, which held neither a beating heart, nor a shadow of a soul, disintegrated into the air, and the holograms of the TPF officers vanished with her, leaving me standing there alone. I walked through the room to the doorway where my father had beckoned me to join writer's workshop. I turned, paused for a brief moment, took in the still silence, and then closed the door to the reading room for the last time.

❧

When I returned to the apartment, the door was ajar, just a crack. Slowly, I pushed it open with my liquidator. Tommy was at school, Anji at a meeting—someone else was here. Without making a sound, I walked down the hallway. Looked into the kitchen. The cabinets were open.

Tommy's bed was turned upside down. His notebook was gone.

And the bedroom. It was as if they had somehow known that this was the room where I was hiding the manuscript. The satin sheets had been thrown to the floor, the apricot-colored perfectly square bedside tables were smashed, Anji's table had been rummaged through, and the box of jewelry was opened. Our closets had been torn apart. Clothes had been pulled out of their proper places and thrown to the floor. I found Anji's salbutamol jacket under a pile of shoes. Where was Anji's Qi now?

I found the laserdriver on the floor under the sleeve

of my sleepsuit. I crawled under the bed with it. I found myself taking a long, deep breath. Then I unscrewed the four nails as quickly as I could, lifted the piece of wood, and looked inside.

I sighed and screwed the piece back into place. I looked around at the mess, and found my eyes staring at the satin sheets on the floor. Underneath them was an outline ... of a man. With my liquidator by my side, I slowly walked toward it. Pointed feet protruded through the sheets on one end and a nose at the other. Clutching my gun with my right hand, I reached down with my left, and pulled off the sheets.

Henry was dead.

"I'm sorry I did this to you," I muttered lamely, looking down at a machine that I had grown attached to. Then I carried him over my shoulder to the building's incinerator. I returned to the apartment, and managed to put almost everything back in its proper place before Anji arrived. I heard her moldable shoes thumping straight to her office, where she closed the door, and undoubtedly escaped to the world of UNICÉ.

I walked out onto the balcony. I took in the smell of lilacs as I stepped onto the green turf. I told it to spin, just for the hell of it. Looking out at the lights of the skyscrapers peeking through the foggy sky, I wondered what the sunsets were like in Norway. I couldn't see them here. The Vales had no other choice. Anji, Tommy, and I had to escape. I was convinced that for ARM, it was for the best too, but if I could manage to successfully deceive Lapin, I wondered, could Sven have been right ... that ARM had a chance in the fight against her? No. Sylvester never wanted violence. He wanted me to write this book.

I took my eyes off the skyscrapers. I tried not to think about the inhabitants of The Mountain where they did all they could to avoid the real world. But so did I. I had to face up to *my* reality. I had to tell Anji the truth.

When I got to her office, the door was unlocked. I came inside and was astounded at what I saw in front of my eyes.

Anji was sitting in her chair, her chin resting on her chest, and a needle hung haphazardly from a vein in her forearm. Standing, facing the desk, with her back to me, was an image of another woman. Her hair was blond and thickly curled, and she wore a shirt with azure and cyan sequins, which covered her scrawny figure. Although I could only see the back of her head, I could make out her arm slowly touching her face and I could hear her whistling a jovial tune.

I slowly walked toward her. As I got closer, I could hear her mumbling to herself but I couldn't understand what she was saying. I took her arm with my hand and her body jumped. Then she turned, slowly, her nose inches from mine. She wore a face that had been altered so many times that although I could tell she was a young lady, she looked like an old woman. She stared at me with shocked eyes. I recognized that hair, her emaciated body—it was the movie star, Kelly Karr. She looked into my face and screamed.

Anji's body gave a violent shudder and the image evaporated along with its scream. Anji lifted her chin, her eyes droopy, mouth crooked. There was an orange glint that had started to form deep in her pupils.

She pulled the needle out of her vein. I took it from her and put it between the vile and the coin-sized nanotron case in the kit on her desk. I held her hand.

"Are you okay?"

She didn't respond.

"I've never *transformed* enough so that the virtual world broke into reality. Only addicts ever … Anji, I thought you were done with this. How often do you *transform*?"

"Not so often," she said, but her eyes shifted to the kit on her desk.

"I can't believe you hid this from me. Anji, you need to stop *transforming*."

"I have to get something," she said, letting go of my hand. She got up from her chair and left the room. I followed her into the bedroom. She went into her closet, shut the door, and locked it. She was hiding herself from me. From the world.

"What is it, Anji?" I spoke through the door. "What's so bad about reality that you have to *transform* all the time?" After a moment, I could hear her start to cry. "I'll help you—"

"It's not *that*!" she yelled between tears.

"Then what is it?"

"I failed Dad. And I failed my son."

"Oh, Anji."

"The Nation thinks my father's immoral. And my son won't fill his shoes."

"There are some things you can't change. You have to accept them as they are. Now open the door."

I heard the door unlock. I pushed it open. Anji was on the ground in a sea of shoes. Tears had fallen onto the sole of a platform pump that she was gripping with both hands. I pulled her up.

"We're in a lot of danger. The case I was working on, it got out of hand. I killed an important man. There will be people coming after us. We need to leave."

"*Leave?*"

"We're going to Norway tomorrow. It's the only place we'll be safe."

"Are you crazy? Look, I'm sure whatever danger it is, you and The Chief can handle it."

"The Chief is no longer our friend. No one is. Except the Creators."

"Creators?!"

I took out the laserdriver, went under our bed, and unscrewed the nails in the floorboard.

"What are you doing?" she asked. "Answer me, Victor!"

I took out the manuscript. It felt heavy.

"This book," I said, "will be read by people all over The City. It will expose the truth."

She looked at me as if I were someone she didn't know. It was then that I realized that while I had lost Anji, she had lost me.

"How *could* you? First, Tommy's drawings, and then *this*." Anji glared at the manuscript as if I were holding the Devil's child. "*You* can go. I'm staying here with Tommy."

"No. You're coming with *me*."

"What do you expect, Victor? For me to just pick up and leave? What about my firm? My father's legacy?"

"We have no other choice! Besides, he'd want you to *live*, Anji. If you stay here, you won't be safe. We've got plenty of money to start over. Just access your account—"

"How about *your* money?"

"I got my bonus. But I'm not going to use it. The bills are stained with blood."

"You *are* crazy."

"All I have to do is finish this book, and then we'll pack up and leave tomorrow."

She looked into my eyes, examining me with her irises. Then she snapped the manuscript from my hands. She jumped out of her chair and ran out of the room. I sprinted after her into the hallway. She stepped onto the balcony, opened the skin of glass, and held the manuscript over the ledge.

"What do you care more about?" she asked, fury in her eyes, as I came onto the balcony. The pages flapped in the wind as she held them in the air. "Your book … or your family?"

"Sylvester Huppington is the head of an underground movement of Creators that I was assigned to expose. That's why I couldn't tell you about the case. You couldn't know that he was a Creator or you would have been in danger."

"So he manipulated you into writing a book? Into caring more about sheets of paper than your own family?"

"He *is* family!"

"What?"

"He's … my real father. His movement was raided yesterday, he had a heart attack, and as he was dying, he told me the truth. He helped me write this book, Anji." I felt choked up, all of a sudden. No. I wouldn't cry. "I'm writing it … for him."

"Oh my God. Sylvester Huppington … is your father?"

"Yes. I can hardly believe it myself."

I looked at Anji's hand gripping the manuscript. It could blow away if she lifted a finger.

"Remember what I told you, Anji. My promise." When I spoke, it was with confidence, with forcefulness, the tone that I used with Anji before we kissed passionately in my office the night we went to The Mountain Theater. It was a voice, a *feeling*, which required me to summon up all the courage in the world. To put aside any shred of doubt, to show that you are responsible husband, strong and good. I only ever used that voice with Anji. Only a woman can make you the man you ought to be.

"I promised you that I would always protect you

and Tommy. That's why we have to leave here. For our safety. I had to write the book for Sylvester. For my father."

Anji pulled the manuscript out of the wind and told the glass to close.

"I guess we both wanted our father's approval so much that we forgot about each other," she said. I started to come to her but she put up her hand. She opened the wooden cover of my manuscript. Her eyes moved across the first page. She read the first and then the second as I stood there in silence.

"Wow," she said. "You're good at this. I never knew there was this side of you."

"I didn't realize it either," I said, taking a step toward her. "All I've wanted is to tell you about it. I wished you could somehow accept it. But you're so occupied with the firm, worrying about Tommy, and *transforming*. I feel like I've lost you. I would give up everything—yes, even the book—if I could have my wife back."

We kissed. She dropped the manuscript into the garden, pages falling between rosemary and forget-me-nots. I slowly placed her in the bed of lilacs. She smiled.

"You don't want your gown?" I asked.

"I don't need it."

With the sound of trickling water, and the scent of lilacs in the air, we made love.

Tommy was sitting at his desk with a marker in his hand. I sat across from him on his bed. "Hey," he said, glumly.

"I'm sorry that they took your notebook."

"It's not just that. I haven't kissed Amber yet. Like

you said, it hasn't been the right moment, but when it comes, I won't let fear get in the way."

"Listen to me. As you know, Dad's job is very dangerous. Something bad happened. We're leaving tomorrow. I don't want you to leave this room 'til then. Not even to go to school."

"But I'll be marked absent. Ms. Hiccup was replaced with an automatron who always knows when we're not there." He paused. "Where are we going?"

"To a better place than here."

I could feel Tommy's tenseness. "But I like it here."

"I know. This is hard. But it's something we have to do. I want you to pack your bags tonight and be ready to leave in the morning. And Tommy, the place we're going … you'll be able to *draw* there."

Tommy didn't say a thing. I could feel his silence. It was going to be hard on him, especially with the new girlfriend. But he'd have to accept it. I got up from the bed and started to go. Then I turned.

"My father—he abandoned me. But I will never leave you. Do you hear me?"

"I know."

"Here," I said, tossing him the apple that Sylvester had given me.

"What's this?"

"So you can taste knowledge. Like Adam did."

❦

I woke up at two in the morning. Anji was snoring peacefully. I got out of bed and gathered the pages of the manuscript from the garden, plucking them from in between basil and lettuce, from under tomatoes and cucumbers. If only I could eat those vegetables, and feel that magical surge of knowledge I was searching for as a child. More than ever, I needed that now.

I went into my office and flipped through the pages. I had developed a thirst for knowledge that could never be quenched. Or maybe that thirst was always there, and I just didn't know it. Maybe it's somewhere in all of us.

I stared at the last page. There I was, forced to finish a story that has yet to end. I was stuck. Lauren wasn't here to help me. Neither was Sylvester. I had to do it alone.

I heard a knock at the door.

"Come in."

It was Anji. She came inside, leaving the door wide open.

"You left it open."

"I know."

"Won't that interrupt the flow of your Qi?"

"I never understood why my father cared for Chinese philosophies."

"Yes, you do. You designed our entire bedroom based on an Eastern philosophy. Remember how you rearranged the furniture when we moved in here? Every object in this house you picked out, and then you chose which room it would go in and where it looked best. You did all the gardening. When the automatrons came to paint the apartment, you told them what color to use."

"So? I wanted the apartment to look nice."

"Well, that was creative, Anji. A friend once told me that everyone has a creative side. You designed this place. You're a Creator too."

"Don't get carried away."

She stood beside me as I gazed at the blank page.

"I'm stuck, Anji. I can't finish."

"Of course you can. Look how much you've written already."

"That doesn't matter. I don't know how to end it."

"When I'm at work, and I have a decision to make, I think about what my father would have done."

My father ... I flipped through my pad, turned the pages. Scanned them with my finger. I came to the words that he had written:

Tap into your subconscious mind. If you get stuck, don't try to fight it. If you're really struggling, close your eyes and clear your mind. The ideas will come.

I shut my eyes. Images flashed through my head. The ceramists sitting at their potter's wheels, outlining their designs with fingers in the air, their eyes darting back and forth as they envisioned their work. Iryna playfully punching Vivek in the chest before drifting over to her sculpture to finish his boxy head. The sensation of my body lifting as I listened to the keys of a piano. The giant canvas in the art room filled with bullet holes. A smashed guitar. Ralph's butterfly with its broken wing. The double chins of the judge shaking as he banned books forever. Sylvester's words, that art can never die. Open.

The restrictions on air flight—the bomb. If we were really the only nation in existence, and books were banned, and the books in the reading room were destroyed, then my book, what you're reading right now, could in fact be ...

I lift my eyes off the last page. I close the book and look down at its wooden cover. I take out the engraver Sylvester gave me with its sharp metal tip. I engrave my name and then write:

The Last Book Ever Written

Chapter Twenty-Four: Norway

It was nine thirty in the morning. I hadn't slept. But my book was nearly complete. I had just finished coloring in the engraving with Tommy's white marker, which I outlined with a black pen, and was about to take the manuscript and put it into my briefcase, but thought I'd leave it on my desk. We didn't have to leave just yet.

I took the liquidator out of the pocket of my nanojacket as a precaution and stuck it underneath my belt. I went to the bedroom. Anji had overslept, but the calm smile across her face told me not to wake her.

I went to Tommy's room to see if he had packed. When he didn't answer my knock on the door, I came inside. The ray of light from the HTD filled the room. His body was in his desk but his mind was gone.

"He left!" I said in disbelief. I widened the lens and stepped into the light, transmitting to Tommy's destination.

Amber's apartment was dark. There were objects strewn on the floor, food left on the living room table next to a pile of drawings. It smelled like banana oatmeal cookies. Amber and Tommy were sitting on the couch, knees touching, a transmittance sensation device attached to Amber's lips.

"Tommy, we need to go *now*!" I shouted. I couldn't

believe that my son would defy me like that.

"*Dad*! Why do you always have to interfere?"

"Why can't you listen to your father?"

"Stay with *me*," Amber commanded. "Your art is here." She lifted one of Tommy's drawings. Attached to it, like a magnet, was a holographic business card. There, on the table, was a stack of cards with the smiling face of Kenneth.

Kenneth ... was Amber's father? This was Kenneth's plot all along—to use his own daughter to manipulate my son! But *why*? I could feel myself trembling as I realized ... he wanted to distract me so he could be alone with Anji.

"Please don't go," Amber was pleading, beginning to cry. "My dad said that he'd hit me if you left." Tommy stood still for a moment. He looked at me and then back at Amber.

"Tommy," I said, looking him straight in the eye. "Your mother is in *danger*."

He turned to Amber. "Bye," he said.

"I'm sorry," Amber replied as we began to transmit. "I liked you. I really did." A tear trickled down her rosy cheek and settled in a small dimple.

We transmitted back to Tommy's room.

"Why didn't you listen to me?" I asked.

"Amber said to come over to her house. That she wanted to try a French kiss. Her dad told her it was okay. So I did what you said—I didn't let fear get in the way, and I went there ... but I shouldn't have done it. It didn't feel right."

"All right. I'm gonna go check in on Mom—"

"WAIT, DAD! You won't be mad anymore when I tell you this—I aced my exams!"

And then I heard Anji scream.

"Stay here," I said to Tommy. "Get into your closet,

lock it, and don't come out. And *listen* to me this time!"

"Okay," Tommy replied, shaking.

I took the liquidator out of my pocket. I jumped out of the doorway, pointing the gun down the hall. The door to my room was open and I could hear movement inside. I was so worried about Anji that I didn't even think about taking my nanojacket for protection. I came closer. I followed Anji's sounds and sprang into the room. Holding my wife, with a gun pointed at her head, was Kenneth.

"I hit him with your blockball bat!" Anji shouted. I could see it sticking out from under the bed. "I got his gun!"

"But you don't have it now, *do* you?" Kenneth snarled, holding the gun.

Anji's sleepsuit had been torn, exposing her upper arm, and as Kenneth held her, she trembled, trying to control her breath. I could see in Kenneth's eyes that he was sad, desperate. I thought about shooting him then and there. But what if I missed?

"Let go of her."

Anji started wheezing. She needed that salbutamol jacket. With my gun pointing at Kenneth, I moved toward the window, circling the room, knowing Kenneth would follow my cue and move as well, in the direction of Anji's closet.

"I taught you how to be a detective," he said. "And then you betrayed me. Was that your plan all along? Learn from me, and then get rid of me so you could take my place?"

"Put the gun down. Don't do something you'll regret."

"I can make plans too, Victor. I'll lure you away, then kill your wife. Then *you'll* take the blame and be kicked off the force. Just like you did to me. And *your* wife will be gone just as mine is now."

"You're sick, Kenneth, using your own daughter to get at my son."

"I made a mistake not killing your wife when I had the chance. I never make the same mistake twice. Spin!" he shouted, and the room spun so that the sun was behind me, creating a glare that reflected off Anji's sleepsuit, blocking my vision. I could make out Anji's face though as Kenneth pulled her toward the closet. Her wheezes were getting worse. She looked down, where the jacket lay stretched on the floor. Kenneth watched her eyes. Then he looked up at me and stepped on the jacket.

"Stop, Kenneth! You don't want to do this!!" Kenneth smiled at the desperation in my voice. Anji was going to die if I didn't do something, the glare, I couldn't shoot, the room spun away from the window, gun pointing at Kenneth, Anji wheezing—

All in an instant, I swung my arm so my liquidator pointed at him, I fired, and so did he. Two streams of water screamed through the air—

Images flooded my mind. The look in Anji's eyes the day I first kissed her, the wetness of her lips. The day Tommy was born, his crumpled up face and squirming body in my arms. The way Tommy smiled at me as he trotted from the end zone back to the dugout after hitting his first home run. Sylvester's words, "you have courage", his wrinkled hand slipping out of mine.

I felt the impact first, my legs out from under me, and I was thrown into the glass window from the force of the gun. It all became a daze, the shards of glass around and inside me, struggling to get to my feet, seeing Kenneth's body motionless on the floor. Then I was putting the jacket around Anji. "Breathe!" I shouted. This wasn't happening. She'll be okay. I put it around her empty face. But she still wasn't breathing.

I ran out of the bedroom. Went into my office. Looked at my desk. At the pages that lay there, the words that spoke the truth, the ink that spilled my emotions, the letters that formed from the deep crevices of my brain and found their way onto the page so that they could crawl with pompous self-indulgence. It's all their fault.

The hall began to spin as I staggered into the kitchen. I felt a sudden pain in my side. I was bleeding.

I didn't care. I gazed across at the kitchen sink. Came to the silver faucet with the shiny handles for hot and cold. I wrapped my fingers around the handles. Turned them on all the way.

I spun back through the hallway and into my office. Took the manuscript. Felt the weight of it in my hands. Into the kitchen. At the sink. Held the manuscript tight. All I could hear was the water coming from the faucet as it hit the bottom of the sink like the crashing of a waterfall. I held up the manuscript. I moved it toward the water—

The TPF officers were right to water the books in the reading room, they knew of the selfishness of creators, who care more about their own pursuits than their family. Creators are no better than those who live for money; we all just care about satisfying ourselves. The only difference is that some people care about green sheets of paper and the others care about white. Yes, I'll destroy the manuscript.

And then my eyes fell on the title. A gust of wind from the running water blew the tops of the pages into the air; they flapped like wings, and I couldn't move them any farther.

"Dad?"

I pulled the manuscript to my side and looked across the room to see Tommy.

"What happened?"

I wanted to tell him that we were going to get to that ship, take Mom with us, and start a new life somewhere else, do what we want to do, not worry about anything, and everything will be okay. I wanted to promise my son that we'd be safe and free and happy. But then the room began to shake and I could hear the whirring of a helicopter over my head.

Epilogue

We waited for him that morning. It didn't take long to realize that something had happened.

Victor was not in his apartment. The only people I saw were a dead man lying in a closet, and an unconscious woman, wrapped in a white jacket. Lying next to the man was a small, golden flute.

I remembered Victor telling me that he hid the manuscript under the floorboards beneath his bed. I found a laserdriver on the bedside table and unscrewed the floorboards one by one. There, hidden in the very center of the room, was the manuscript.

It was then that I received a message from Sara. They needed to leave right away. I sent an anonymous message for an emergency vehicle to be sent to Victor's apartment. I rushed to the ship and was the last person on board. I took my brother's manuscript. *This* book, the one he wrote with father.

I am now safely in Norway with Sara and many of the remaining members of ARM. I'm writing this here, as I gaze across a fjord at snow-capped mountains. I like to walk to waterfalls, close my eyes, and listen to the sound of falling water, taking in the scent of fresh air, the cool breeze whipping against my face. In these moments, I believe that some things can never be destroyed by man.

But people will always invent. There is nothing stopping them, even as people become less human, until they become the inventions themselves.

Sometimes I take walks around the fjords. Water can be so peaceful and calm yet so dangerous and powerful. Like technology, it can create but also destroy. There is plenty of water in this place. But that is all. I hike the mountains, searching for a footprint, the billowing of smoke from a fire, a scrap of food, any evidence of human existence. We are the only ones here.

I remember that day when I was just a young girl. Weinstein was in my father's office. Lapin is developing a bomb that could wipe out the entire planet, he said. Well, it nearly happened, and we hardly noticed. We were gone from the earth a long time ago, far away in outer dimensions of UNICÉ, between the images of our televisions and computer screens. We did not try to make the world a better place until it was too late.

Sven stayed behind. He's been sending me cryptic messages on UNICÉ. From what I can gather, Victor's wife is in a coma in a hospital somewhere in The City. Of course I know now that the woman I saw in Victor's apartment was his wife. She was beautiful.

Victor's son has been put in a foster home. His adoptive parents are Upperclassmen. The father is a stockbroker and the mother a banker. He's returned to school and is applying to high schools with good business programs. I don't know if he still draws. Sven wanted to recruit him for ARM, but I adamantly refused. He's only thirteen years old.

No one knows what happened to Victor. There was a news report on UNICÉ about Dallas Grumm's only daughter, stating that Victor was the man responsible for his wife's condition. We hold out hope that he'll turn up one day at Huppington Books. But I know that if he is alive, he's most likely behind bars.

Wherever you are, Victor, you will never be forgotten.

If I were to publish Victor's manuscript on UNICÉ, and were somehow able to get by cyber security, it would still be censored. So I'm keeping it as a paper book, the way I believe he would have wanted. I'm sending it via ship and have coordinated with Sven, who has vowed to distribute it as a catalyst for his rebellion. He told me that if he succeeds in overthrowing the President, and a new society is born, this would be the first book ever written.

I hope that this is what you would have wanted, Victor, for me to complete your manuscript in this way. I know that your legacy, our father's legacy, and that of all Creators, will live on.

Before sending your manuscript to Sven, I opened it for one last look. I saw, flying out of its pages, with black spots along its yellow back, and brisk fluttering wings, the image of a yellow butterfly.